TWISTED INDULGENCE

TWISTED INDULGENCE

A BODYGUARD AGE GAP NOVELLA

Nichole Steel

an imprint of Nicole Frail Books, LLC
Avoca, Pennsylvania

Attic and Attic Ebooks are imprints of Nicole Frail Books, LLC, with offices located in Avoca, Pennsylvania, USA.

For permission requests, write to permissions@nicolefrailbooks.com. To purchase copies of this book in bulk or to stock in your brick-and-mortar stores, please write to sales@nicolefrailbooks.com. For publicity requests or other inquiries, or to get in touch with the author or publisher, write to info@nicolefrailbooks.com.

Cover design by Covers by Sophie
Section break single rose design by wowow/Canva; QR code rose design by julia425139304/Canva
Edited & Typeset by Nicole Frail/Nicole Frail Edits, LLC
First publication: April 2025

Learn more about the publisher at:
www.nicolefrailbooks.com | @nicolefrailbooks
www.attic-ebooks.com | @attic.ebooks
www.andyoupress.com | @andyoupress

Print ISBN: 978-1-965852-42-2
Ebook ISBN: 978-1-965852-41-5

To those who love with their whole hearts.
It's your strength.

TRIGGER WARNINGS

Kidnapping, torture (side character and not describe other than physical appearance after), threats of death and bodily harm, physical fighting, stalking, descriptive open-door sex scenes, virgin FMC, oral sex, cursing, and gun violence.

CHAPTER 1

RACHEL

SWEAT BEADS DOWN MY FOREHEAD, and my muscles burn from the strain, but I'm not giving up this fight. Not yet. I whirl my leg around as I try to land a blow to his jaw. He blocks it with his forearm, knocking me slightly off balance.

Seeing his opportunity, he lunges forward and wraps his legs around me, trapping me. He takes me to the mat and pain shoots through my body.

"Ahh!" I bellow in frustration.

"Tap out, Rach." Mark grunts through labored breaths.

I twist and thrash my body, trying to break free, but it only gives him the perfect opening. He hooks his arm under mine and forces his arm into my throat with lethal pressure. *What a rookie mistake.*

"Tap!" Mark orders as he holds strong.

I'm unable to breathe.

Resolved to the loss, I tap his arm twice and he immediately releases me.

I gasp for air, and between inhalations, I manage to get out: "I thought I had you this time!"

Frustration weighs heavy in my chest as my heartbeat slows and I try to catch my breath.

"Sorry, not today." He laughs and offers his hand to help me up.

I can't believe I let him get the chokehold. I'm better than that.

Once I'm out of the ring, I take a long drag of my water bottle and the coolness is both soothing and a punch in the gut.

Under normal circumstances, MMA fighters would train with their same gender, but I need to be able to beat any man in my path. Men rule this world and think they can take whatever they want in it. But they can't have me . . . not anymore.

Mark strides over to me, his grin victorious and gloating, which is not unusual for him, and I roll my eyes at the sight. We have been pairing off and sparring a few times a week since I started. He's become a good friend and gym partner.

"So, any fun plans this evening?" he asks as I remove

my hand wraps and mouth guard, grab my sweat towel, and stuff them all into my gym bag.

"No, not unless you count a good book and bubble bath. You?"

"Not really." The uncertainty in his tone drags my attention away from my bag to him. He shifts on his feet only slightly and rubs his hand over his chiseled jawline. "I was actually wondering if you would like to grab dinner and maybe hit a bar after?"

Mark and I have hung out socially before, but usually it's always with a group. This sounds different. Almost like he's asking me on a date, but he's just a good friend, and I have no intention of changing that.

"Oh, yeah. We could ask Jake, Shelly, Max, and Tyler to join, too! I bet the Blue Canary has a band tonight since it's Friday." Hopefully this is what he was thinking, and if not, maybe he'll take the bait.

"That would be fun, but not what I meant." He pauses and runs a hand through his short, blonde hair. "Rachel, I want to take you out on a date."

My stomach sours at the confirmation.

Mark is a great guy. He's fun, sweet, and a wonderful training partner who never goes easy on me. But I know that's all he'll ever be to me.

Anxiety swirls inside my chest. I don't want to lose the friendship we have, and I have no idea how to deny him.

I've been asked out three times in my life and have

said yes all three times. And each relationship ended worse than the one before.

The first two I figured out were only interested in gaining points with my dad—the head of the largest gang in Los Angeles, the Night Stalkers—and the last one was part of a scheme that led to my kidnapping three years ago. It's safe to say that guy's dead now.

So, here I am, a twenty-two-year-old woman without a clue how to reject the man standing in front of me—and do it in a way that won't impact our friendship or my training.

The silence is starting to stretch, and it's becoming uncomfortable. Mark is staring at me, waiting for my answer, and my brain feels muddled as I try to sort out what to say or do.

My eyes dart over to my bodyguard, Daniel, who is leaning against the doorframe of the gym's entrance, watching me, and before I can think otherwise, I blurt, "I really appreciate the offer, but Daniel and I are actually seeing each other now."

Mark's hopeful and smiling expression instantly drops, and his mouth presses into a firm line as his body goes rigid.

Crap. I wanted to avoid hurting him, but I seem to have only created a different problem.

"Really? You're dating your bodyguard, and your dad is good with that?" His tone is clipped and sharp in a way I've never heard from him before, and my anxiety spikes again. His eyes shift over to Daniel, and he shoots him a glare before returning to me.

I try reassuring him with a smile and keep my tone even and calm when I say, "Of course he is."

"Huh. Daniel never mentioned anything at poker night. I guess I'll see you later." Mark's eyes are pinned on Daniel and irritation is rolling off him in waves. He doesn't wait for my response. He throws his bag over his shoulder and heads straight for Daniel.

Double crap.

CHAPTER 2

DANIEL

ONE MINUTE RACHEL IS GETTING her ass handed to her by Mark, and next thing I know, he's marching over to *me* with fury burning in his eyes. I stand straight and adjust my suit jacket, mentally preparing for whatever is about to unfold.

Mark and I have been friends for a while now and used to work together at a club downtown before I took the job as Rachel's personal bodyguard after a kidnapping incident. I know my friend well enough to tell when his intentions are less than civil.

"What the hell, man?" He stands in front of me and tosses his bag to the ground. "You want to explain why you're breaking the biggest rule in the book and didn't even care enough to tell me?"

I'm so confused right now, but I don't show it. The rule he's referring to is "You don't touch the client," and somehow, he thinks I got involved with Rachel. This is a huge accusation. A career-ending one.

Bodyguards in the industry have dated their clients from time to time, and when it ends badly, they lose their jobs and then are blacklisted because they can't be trusted to keep their hands to themselves.

"Mark, I have—" I'm cut short when Rachel runs up, wraps her arm around my waist, and places a hand on my chest. I instantly stiffen at her touch.

"It's okay, sweetie, I told him about us. I'm sorry I didn't give you a heads-up first." Her voice is honeyed, and warning bells ring in my head.

I know Mark wouldn't threaten or hurt her in any way, so why the facade right now? Something happened that I obviously missed, and my duty is to Rachel.

Time to put on a show, and all I can say is she better have a good reason for this.

I plaster an adoring smile on my face when I look down at her and then turn back to Mark. "Sorry I didn't tell you sooner, but things just happened. I'll tell you more at poker on Sunday."

"Whatever, man. I told you things. I trusted you, and then you go and pull this behind my back." Mark steps into my space now, and I push Rachel behind me slightly. We can't have this conversation right now.

He's mad about more than just me potentially

messing up my career. Two weeks ago at poker, he confessed he has strong feelings for Rachel. He wanted my permission to pursue her because I've mentioned having feelings for her in the past, but I could never pursue her, so I encouraged him to ask her out. He thinks I've betrayed him. And that's certainly what it looks like.

"Mark, I'm sorry. I promise to explain on Sunday." I'm pleading with him now. I don't want to get into a fight with him over something that I don't even fully understand.

He shakes his head and then backs up, grabbing his bag. "You're supposed to be my friend, but I'm glad to see you sealed the deal yourself." He snarls and shoves past me, then heads straight out the door.

I can't blame him for his anger; it looks like I set him up to be humiliated.

I turn my attention to the woman who has made one hell of a mess for me. She has an arm crossed protectively over her chest and is nervously picking at her lip.

"I'm sorry that he was so upset about that, but what did he mean by you sealing the deal?"

"Never mind that. Go get your stuff. We're leaving, and you're going to explain whatever that was. Then we will discuss what we're going to do about it."

This is great, just great. Boundaries have clearly been crossed with my client, my friend and colleague thinks I've betrayed him, and to top it all off, this could destroy my career.

I feel frozen—for the first time, I don't have an answer. When things get dangerous, it's always cut and dry. Simple. Just make a decision. Her safety is always the priority.

This is different. . . .

"What is there to do about it? It's over now. We don't have to do anything."

"Oh, you have no idea the can of worms you just opened. Bag. Car. Now," I order.

She rolls her eyes but walks away to collect her bag.

Following behind her, I watch intently as she slides her sweatpants over her shorts and pulls her auburn hair from its bun, allowing it to fall just above her shoulders.

Rachel has always been gorgeous with a sweet and fun personality to go with her looks, but her eyes are my favorite. Her sea-blue eyes remind me of the best summer day, with the ocean crashing along the beach and the total peace it brings. It's always surprised me how little she dates. Even now, sweaty and in need of a shower, her beauty still draws me in.

She snaps up with her hands on her hips and then gestures one hand toward the door. "We going or what?"

She's always got so much attitude when she's frustrated, and she's the one who got us into this mess in the first place.

I turn and lead the way, not giving her the curtesy

of a response. She is following close behind—I can feel her energy, sense her presence there. It's a little unnerving that I don't even have to check to know she's there. Thankfully, it's a quick walk through the gym to the car. I open the door for her to climb into the passenger seat and take her bag to the trunk, just like always.

How the hell am I going to get out of this without destroying my career or ending up dead at her father's hand? I highly doubt he would appreciate even a rumor of my hands being on his daughter, even if it's all a lie.

I feel so tense my shoulders are starting to ache. I roll my neck before climbing into the driver's seat to bring us back to the Hudson Estate. The tension in this car is not helping my anxious, stressed energy, and Rachel only sits silently.

"So, are you going to explain why I had to pretend we're together?" I snap unintentionally.

"Well, Mark asked me out, and I'm not interested in being anything other than training partners and friends."

I grip the wheel hard enough my knuckles are turning white. She put so much at risk for a date denial?

"I just didn't know how to say no to him. I've never rejected someone before. I've always managed to avoid the awkwardness of a solid no, and I tried that with him and it wasn't working. Then I saw you and thought it was an easy out."

"You thought it was an easy out?" Anger is coursing

through me, but I got a handle on it long ago, so she won't see it. "He is livid with me, Rachel, and you want me to what? Tell him in two days' time that we broke up? How would I explain still having a job?"

She huffs in frustration and crosses her arms over her chest. "Sure, tell him whatever you want, Daniel. I don't care."

"No. We have to fix this. Do you not understand that my career is on the line here?" I don't mean to start yelling at her, but I do. "When bodyguards date their clients and they break up, they typically lose their jobs and are seen as un-hirable because they can't be trusted to keep their hands to themselves!"

"I didn't realize it was this big of a deal, okay!" She yells back and slams her hand onto the center console. "Let's-let's just go out on a fake date or something and then have a nice, clean breakup. You could say you came to your senses before anything became too serious, and we agreed to keep things professional. Tell him it was only one date and nothing more, okay?"

That could work. Mark will no doubt run through the streets that I'm dating Rachel, but . . . with evidence of only the one date and a clean split after, my reputation will still be damaged but should be salvageable, especially if I continue to work as her guard.

"Fine, I'll take you out, and we'll take photos for evidence. That won't fix my friendship with Mark, but I'll deal with that. If your dad catches wind of this, you will explain this was all *your* doing. Hopefully this will fix things with the least amount of damage possible."

"Okay, I guess that's fair. I'll dress nice, and you can take all the photos you want, and you can say whatever you need to. Please just don't tell anyone it's all a show. I-I don't want to become a laughingstock." The sadness in her request is almost physical.

Instantly, I feel myself soften to her.

I sigh. "Fine. Tomorrow?"

"Sounds great." She sneers and turns her back to me, staring out the window.

I rake a hand through my hair and note the ball of anxiety in my chest. This is the best decision. I keep my job and reputation, and I'll just have to make sure to keep my mouth shut from now on. Going on a date with her won't be any different than escorting her to her various activities and outings.

Who cares that I'm about to fake date not only my client, but a girl who is way too young for me.

The same girl I've been pining after for far too long.

CHAPTER 3

RACHEL

HOW AM I GOING ON a date with hot and all-too-tempting Daniel? He is like a million-dollar piece of art behind a glass case: you never get to touch it, only admire from a distance. Somehow, though, I was just given permission to get dangerously close.

Daniel has always been hot as hell itself. I've imagined running my fingers through his thick, brown hair, feeling his body on mine, kissing his pillowed lips and feeling his stubbled facial hair . . . and more than once I've felt his soul-searching, forest green eyes on me, watching in ways one could probably deem inappropriate.

I've been crushing on Daniel for a while now, but boundaries have been strictly upheld. I could never say I had a crush on my bodyguard because my dad would have gotten me a new one, and I would have been ridiculous for chasing a man fifteen years older than me. I never want to lose Daniel, so I've been happy with the professional relationship we've had, but today those boundaries got a bit blurry.

After the gym, Daniel brought me back to my family's estate where I live in the cottage on the west side, per my father's mandate. He has many enemies, so moving into an apartment or dorm for college was out of the question. He almost didn't let me go to college at all, but with Daniel at my side, he relented, agreeing that my education was important. Hopefully, after undergrad, I'll be able to get into medical school and become a doctor. My dream is to help those who may not have access to normal medical care because of their profession. Gang members and Mafia men need medical care, too, right?

"Thank you . . . and I'm sorry for making such a mess for you, Daniel," I say as I climb from the car. He joins me and walks me to the door. My heart wants to see it as a romantic gesture, but the reality is that it's just part of the job. He'll see me inside and then will stay to guard the house.

He pauses at the door as I walk in, and I stare at him, confused. He shifts on his feet with his hands in his pockets. "I'm not staying today. I'll inform Rob that you're back, and he will handle your security. I'll be back tomorrow."

My chest aches slightly and guilt washes over me. He's really upset with me if he isn't staying. Daniel was hired to be my mobile security, while Rob and the team are the estate's security. Daniel always just preferred to spend the days with me. Since I've been his client, this is only the third time he has chosen to leave me with the other security detail for the day.

I step forward, desperate to fix whatever I've broken. "You don't have to. I'm so sorry I made a mess, but we'll fix it, and it will all be like nothing happened," I plead.

"I'm not upset. I just need some space to think. You have a great rest of the day, and I'll see you tomorrow."

He doesn't wait for me to respond. He closes the door with me inside, and I watch as he walks across the lawn to the guards' booth.

I guess blurring lines had more than one unintended consequence, and the ache I feel in my chest is downright crippling.

Turning and pressing my back to the door, I blow out a breath. It may only be the afternoon, but I need wine and girl talk. I pull out my phone and scroll down to Meg's text thread.

> Come over. It's a wine-
> mergency.

> Are we talking the light rosé or
> the merlot?

> Neither....
> We need sangria.

> **Shit. We're getting drunk. Be there
> in two hours with supplies.**

Meg is literally a life saver, and I've been able to count on her as my ride or die since middle school. If I ever get arrested, I have no doubt that Meg will either be in that holding cell with me or posting bail. She's one of those friends who knows all of my secrets but would die to keep them. I don't have a sister, just my older brother Simon, so Meg is the closest thing I've got.

I decide it's time to abandon the door and walk to the kitchen to make a cup of strawberry tea with honey. Meg will be here in two hours, and for now, I just need to distract myself from all the emotions swirling around.

Armed with a hot cup of tea, I plop down on the couch where my computer is along with the outrageous number of textbooks thrown about. I have a paper due for biology class next Thursday and that should keep me occupied until Meg arrives. Why papers are required for science classes is beyond me, but I must write them to pass the class regardless.

I pore over my books, tap away at my computer until my brain is utterly fried, and then go shower and change just in time for Meg to walk through my front door.

"Rach! I'm here and armed with booze!" she yells to announce her arrival.

I move my computer and mountain of books from the couch to the floor off to the side before meeting her. My saving grace is here. Homework is mostly done. Now, it's time to drink and forget the feelings that still hang heavy on my shoulders.

"Hey!" I yell back. "I'll meet you in the kitchen."

She makes it there before I do, and I hear the clanking of bottles.

"You're a life saver," I say as I approach her and pull my cutting board down from the cupboard to start slicing the fruit.

"I know." She shrugs unapologetically and I chuckle a little, shaking my head. She has never been a humble woman. Hell, some days she's cocky enough to put some men's egos to shame.

I reach for the bags and take in the spread of items on the counter. Red wine, rum, strawberries, an orange, a lemon, a red apple, and a small bouquet of roses.

"What's with the flowers?" I nod toward them.

Flowers aren't an ingredient for sangria, at least not one I've ever had. I grab the fruit to start slicing, and Meg starts fishing out my pitcher from the cabinet across the kitchen.

"They were on your porch with a small envelope. I just brought them in. Hah! Got the pitcher. Next time this needs to be at the front for easy access," she teases, but I'm no longer paying attention.

My confusion is thick. Those stupid flowers have stolen my focus.

Maybe Daniel left the flowers to let me know I'm forgiven? He's the only one I can think of who would leave anything on my porch and have the access to do it. Rob or the other guards would have handed them to me directly.

Meg walks over with the pitcher in hand, and I toss in the fruit before heading to the flowers. Six red roses wrapped in white tissue paper. Just inside is a small envelope, and I waste no time ripping it open.

Why has Daniel sent me flowers? He obviously did it discreetly so the other guards wouldn't know. A nervous energy has me fumbling around, taking longer than it should to reveal a plain, white card.

> *Counting the minutes until*
> *I hold you in my arms*
> *—Your Special Someone*

Reading the note, my heart sinks just a little. This *was* Daniel, but not because I'm forgiven or because he cares. No, these were sent as part of our fake dating game.

I feel my face fall, and the sadness and guilt from earlier make an unwelcome return to the forefront of my mind. Meg rips the card from my hands before I even realize she'd come over.

"Who is this *Special Someone* you failed to tell me about, and why does a romantic gesture like this have you on the brink of tears?" She places both hands on her hips, full attitude on display. She raises both eyebrows, urging me to spill.

"It's nothing, Meg, and the flowers were not sent for the reason you think." I drop my gaze from hers then grab the pitcher of sangria and head back to the couch.

Meg releases a frustrated huff while grabbing the wine glasses and quickly catches up to me.

"I'm going to need more detail than that, Rachel. Is this why you called for a wine-mergency? For this *Special Someone*?"

"Mark asked me out at the gym today—"

"And you said yes? I thought you didn't even think he was good looking?"

"Girl, shut up and let me explain." She wants to know what's going on so bad but won't shut her mouth long enough for me to even tell her.

I take a deep breath and tell her the whole story. How I panicked at rejecting Mark, then how upset he was, all the way to the doorway where Daniel left me for the day. She listens with sympathy in her eyes and refills my glass as needed.

"So let me get this straight. You blew off Mark, made a big mess for Daniel, and now you guys have to go on a fake date only to call it off and remain professional? Wow, girl, way to go." She isn't being sarcastic. She smiles at me before sipping from her glass.

Why is she cheering me on right now? I have potentially ruined the little relationship I have with Daniel, and she's praising me?

I lean forward on my knees. "Why are you happy about this?"

"Why aren't you?" She cheers like it's obvious why I should be. "You have had a crush on Daniel ever since his first year here, and now he's going to wine and dine you and maybe even kiss you. Who cares if it's not real? Rachel, for one night you get to have the guy you've been pining over for literal *years*."

Putting it in those terms, she's not wrong. The idea of kissing Daniel has butterflies erupting in my belly and heat flooding my cheeks.

"You're blushing just thinking about him. You've got it so bad," Meg teases, and I punch her in the arm.

"So what if I do?" I tease back, a smile forming on my face.

This is why I called for a wine-mergency. Meg brings me perspective and hope in situations where I don't see any. She can make me smile when joy feels miles away. Plus, we both get drunk off our asses, which always makes for an even better night.

Hours pass, and after killing the pitcher, more gossip

and teasing, and a rough round of living room karaoke, it's high time for bed and I'm thankful for it.

"You just want to sleep over, or should I call Rob to get you a ride home?"

"Snuggles in bed, pleeease."

I love Drunk Meg. She is so much more dramatic than Sober Meg.

"Okay, I'll meet you in there."

She fumbles through my living room and down the hall to my bedroom. She's way farther gone than I am.

I grab the pitcher and glasses and take them to the kitchen. The flowers are still on the counter. My chest swells at the sight of them. Who cares that it's all fake? I pick up the flowers and deeply inhale their fresh scent. Just for one day I'll allow myself to enjoy Daniel as if it were real and then I'll lick my wounds later.

I pull a vase down from the cabinet, fill it with water, and arrange the flowers just right so every flower is visible. I walk it to the dining room table and set in the center. Tonight, I'll imagine that the message in the card is true.

When I reach my bedroom, Meg is already passed out, and I join her big spoon, little spoon–style. This was a perfect way to end a day with a hard start, and tomorrow I can call the man I desire mine, if only for a little while.

CHAPTER 4
DANIEL

SHE WAS SO UPSET. I NEARLY broke in two staring into her pleading eyes while she was begging me to stay, to not be upset with her. I was honest when I said I wasn't upset with her, but I couldn't stay. Repairing things with Mark was too heavy of a weight in my mind to not address immediately.

After leaving her place, I get on the road and head straight to Mark's apartment. I have no idea what I'll say to him, but I have to try. We have worked in this industry together for the past five years, and we have been good friends for almost four of those. I don't want this to be the thing that destroys our friendship.

I pull into his building's parking garage and take a moment to think. How am I going to do this? If I tell him the truth, it will ruin the friendship he has with Rachel and most certainly make her into a joke at the gym. Mark has a habit of being petty when he's hurt, and I need to protect Rachel from that if I can.

I could tell him it wasn't planned, and it just happened, but he would probably call bullshit on that. I rub my hand over my jaw and my head starts to ache from the stress of it all.

Another car is pulling into the garage now. A red Toyota with a bumper sticker that reads: *If you're reading this, be prepared to kiss it.*

I recognize it instantly as Mark's personal vehicle. He must have had some errands to run for me to beat him here.

He climbs out of his car still wearing his gym clothes as I climb out of mine.

"Hey, man!" I yell, catching his attention, and something bristles in me, but I ignore it. There's so much wrong with this whole thing, of course I would feel off. "I'm hoping we can talk for a minute."

He drops his head, shaking it, and tosses his bag onto the roof of his car. He squares his stance and crosses his arms over his chest as I approach to him, and I keep my guard up. He's still angry, and I would be too if the roles were reversed.

"You got balls of steel or something, man?" His gaze locks with mine.

"I'm just here to talk. I'm sorry about how things

went down at the gym. I want to work this out; we've been friends for too long not to."

"That's rich coming from you." His voice turns dangerously low, sounding off every warning bell in my head. "I've worked in your shadow for the past five years, taking the jobs you were too good for." He steps forward, entering my space, but I don't move. "And now you humiliate me by telling me to pursue a woman who's already with you."

He pushes me, but I don't budge. A low rumble vibrates in my throat, emanating from the restraint not to beat the hell out of him. Mark may be younger than me, but with age comes experience, and I still have a few inches on him along with an extra fifty pounds of muscle. If this is the way he wants this to go down, I won't be intimidated by him.

"That's not how it happened, and I heard what you said. You're right—it will destroy my career. I'll call things off tomorrow after our date. We *just* started, so it won't be an issue to go back to a professional relationship."

"Too fucking late. I'm done. I deserve the jobs, the girl, the life I want!" He steps back, rolling his shoulders and taking a deep breath.

I watch closely as he turns to grab his bag from the roof of his car where he'd set it earlier, fully aware of every movement he makes.

"You enjoy that date tomorrow and be thankful for

everything you have because you never know when it all might just disappear." His voice is deep, menacing.

If he's threatening her, I'll drop him in this garage here and now.

"Are you making threats against my client?" I snarl at him and step forward.

"I'd never threaten Rachel. Just telling you to be thankful is all." A wicked smile crosses his face before he turns to the elevator.

I don't move, watching every one of his movements until the doors slide closed. Once he's gone, I jog to my car. He said he wasn't threatening Rachel, but I need to know for sure. The rage in my head and the anxiety in my chest won't allow me to ignore even the slightest possibility.

I knew reconciling with Mark was going to be difficult, but I didn't think he would respond that way. I make my way to the car and whip out my phone as soon as I'm seated. I dial Rob's number.

"What's wrong?"

I never call unless it's urgent.

"Is Rachel safe? Had any visitors since I've left?"

"She's in her cottage, and Miss Panko arrived less than a half hour ago. No one else in or out."

"You're sure?"

"Yes. Is there something the team needs to be aware of, Daniel?"

My answer should be yes. They need to know that

Mark is on edge and has possibly made a threat against Rachel. I doubt he'll do anything, but I can't know for sure. But if I say yes, they will also alert Mr. Hudson, and he'll want to know what caused the shift. I'm not prepared to answer those questions, not yet. We have to go on this date to keep Rachel's hands clean and then call it off for me.

"No. I've dealt with it. I just needed to be sure on your end."

"Okay. Let me know if things change on your end, and I'll do the same." He ends the call with no response from me.

I pull out of the garage and onto the busy main road and head for my apartment near the Hudson Estate. Over the years, Rachel's become everything that is important to me, and if something happened, I don't know how I could ever live with that. Rob said she was fine, and if history has proven anything, she's most likely drinking with Megan.

The fifteen-minute drive does nothing to settle me. The unease still eats at me as I arrive home. Every fiber of me wants to go back to her place and make sure for myself that she's safe, but I can't. Things are messy enough as it is, and I need to work out all these feelings so I can lock them away for tomorrow.

I make no moves to settle in. Instead, I cross the kitchen to the stairs that lead to the basement. I flick on the overhead light and turn on the sound system so my rock playlist starts. Next, I toss my shirt to the floor and hit the weight bench. Working out until my muscles quake and sweat has drenched every inch of me has always been the best way to clear my head and help me get a handle on my emotions. Tonight will be no different.

Good morning. Do you I need to
escort you anywhere today?

I have no plans today.
Meg spent the night.

I'll be there at six to pick you up.
Dress nice. We're going to Pontera's.

Isn't Pontera's super fancy?
This is just for show remember,
no need to get crazy.

Yes, it's a nice place and somewhere I
would take you if it were a real date.
Remember, you started this
whole charade.

I'm thankful I don't have to see her before our date. Somehow, I would've had to act normal, like nothing is happening, and I don't think I could've. This woman has had me in a chokehold for far too long, but no matter how hard I've tried, I can't rid myself of the desire to make her mine.

I set my phone on my desk and roll my shoulders. I don't usually get anxious, but ever since this all started, I haven't fully shaken it.

With Rachel not needing me today, I pull out files on people Mr. Hudson has asked me to look into for him. They are non-urgent because he knows how busy his daughter is, but the files have been sitting here for a week and a half now, and it's a welcome distraction.

First up is Peter Malvo. Age twenty-five. Born in New Jersey to a single mother. Moved to L.A. last year and started apprenticing as a business intern at Mirage Tower last month.

Ever since Rachel was taken by Mr. Hudson's biggest rival, he has made it his mission to know everything about everyone who is working at the Mirage Tower. It's the front company of the Crimson Bears, the second largest gang in L.A. and the one that is always seeking ways to bring down Mr. Hudson and the Night Stalkers.

I note nothing of significance about this other than a rose obsession and a stalking charge from five years ago, but I can't find anything tying him to the Bears. That could just mean they haven't recruited him yet.

Still, as I stare at his photos, something in my gut tells me there's more to this guy than meets the eye.

I place all the details in his file and mark it as one to watch simply because something's there—I just haven't found it yet. No way would the Bears have brought in a business intern with a felony stalking charge without some plan for him.

One down, five to go, and then it's time to take Rachel out. I want nothing more than for this to be real, but it can never be. That fact alone makes me want to pull out all the stops tonight. If I'll only get her for a few hours, I'm going to make the most of it. Now, I just need to keep myself in check and not do anything I'll regret.

I stand outside Rachel's cottage, trying to keep my frustration at bay. This whole thing has crossed so many boundaries already. Any other time, I would just walk in because, as her bodyguard, I'm entitled to such privileges, but right now I'm her "date," and I would never just walk into a date's home without being invited in.

Fuck it. This whole thing is a sham anyway.

Once inside, I spot her textbooks and school supplies thrown about. It's just another reminder that she's a young college student and I'm a damn cradle robber for even being interested.

"Rachel, it's six. Are you ready to go?" I yell while shifting on my feet uncomfortably. God, how did I ever think this was a good idea? It seemed like a quick and easy fix, but the longer this goes on, the more I find myself questioning that decision. My feelings were easy to keep locked away with her at a distance, and now tonight I have to hold her close the way I've imagined doing many times. If I'm not careful, those feelings may open up and swallow me whole.

A moment later, she emerges from her bedroom and my mouth instantly dries. *Holy shit.* I've seen this woman dressed up for a party, a date, etcetera, many times. But tonight, she's beyond beautiful. Her auburn hair is down with loose curls. Makeup complements her features and make her eyes deep and her lips tempting.

She stands there, allowing my eyes to rake over her. A soft smile forms on her lips and her cheeks pinken as I take her in. The dress she's wearing is lavender. It's a tight top with a slight V, showing just enough of her tits to be tasteful and tempting at the same time. The skirt flows gracefully over her hips, stopping just above her knees, and her heels pull it all together. She is the most beautiful woman I've ever seen.

"Wow . . . you look absolutely breathtaking." I step toward her, and she rubs her hands down her dress.

"Thank you. You look pretty good yourself," she says in return.

What the hell do I do now? I've been in near-death situations easier than this. The anxious energy and the tension are growing with every passing second as her words linger in the air. I feel like I'm holding a grenade with the pin pulled and this could blow up in my face at any given moment.

I clear my throat and decide to jump straight in headfirst. "Okay, rules and expectations." I need some level of control in this. "We'll go to dinner. Take a cute selfie together like you normally would. Hold hands if we see anyone we know. And at the end of the night, we'll find someone to take a picture of us. Now, no touching unless necessary, no talking about this being fake, and after—"

"Jesus, Daniel." She cuts me off and I feel my eyes grow wide. "Just relax. This can be fun if you allow it, and I'd like fun because it's been a while since I've been on a date." She throws her hands on her hips in exacerbation.

Fuck. I'm already screwing this up. This isn't even real and I'm being a controlling asshole. This shit is why no woman wants to be with me . . . not to mention, many have an issue with the line of work I'm in.

I sigh. "I'm sorry. Normally, I have to go through everything with a fine-toothed comb and plan for anything that could go wrong. This whole situation has me feeling a little on edge. I just need some control."

She steps closer to me and places her hand on my chest. It sends a shiver through me, and even though it's something so small, I know I'll crave it tomorrow.

She looks up at me and holds my gaze. "Let me share some of the weight on this."

There's a long pause, and as I feel the fucking current pulling us toward one another, all I can think of is how many more lines we're crossing.

I step back from her. "Are you ready to go? I would hate to miss our reservation."

Her face falls slightly, but only for a moment. Did I hurt her? The thought makes my stomach turn.

"Yes, let's get this over with." Her words punch me in the gut, and I know I deserved it.

There's no way she didn't feel the same pull I did, and like the rule-following coward I am, I stepped away from it.

CHAPTER 5

RACHEL

I'VE SEEN PHOTOS OF PONTERA'S in magazines and on television, but my God, it's even better in person. Above us hang crystal chandeliers with low lighting, round tables throughout the room are covered in black tablecloths and topped with tall, flickering candles, and across the room a pianist plays soft music in front of a low, burning fireplace.

If Daniel wanted to fake the romance for the evening, he certainly chose the right place to do it. This place screams intimacy to its very core. I knew he was all-in this evening as soon as he walked through my door. He wasn't wearing his usual suit, but rather a button-down white shirt with the sleeves rolled up to his forearms, revealing tattoos I have never seen before, making him all the sexier. Plus khaki pants that show off his muscular backside and thighs. The way this man looks tonight has every inch of me craving his touch and desperate to see if has any more hidden tattoos, but it will never happen, so I lock it away deep inside. We're just playing pretend.

"Welcome to Pontera's. Do you have a reservation?" the hostess asks when we approach the stand.

"Yes, for Daniel Taylor."

"Perfect, right this way." She smiles and leads the way to our table.

Daniel places his hand on my lower back, and my breathing hitches from the intimate gesture. Butterflies fill my stomach.

We follow the hostess through the restaurant to the side of the room closest to the pianist and fireplace, and I'm in awe every step of the way. Every table is filled with guests dressed to the nines like we are, and we are seated at a corner booth, slightly in the shadows, providing even more of a romantic feel.

Daniel gestures for me to sit. "At your service, mam." He says this when we are in public to keep proper boundaries and edict, but the soft smile and the sparkle in his eyes tells me he isn't trying to be professional this time, but a gentleman.

I take my seat, and he walks to his side of the table, moving in close, yet far enough not to crowd me, just as a waiter dressed in a full black suit with a white tie appears next to us.

"Good evening, my name is Michael, and I will be taking care of you this evening. What can I get you to drink?"

"Two glasses of your Mondavini Red Reserve please," Daniel says when his eyes lock onto mine. It's his job to know me, but this evening he has brought me to the best restaurant in the state and ordered my favorite—but also expensive—wine. Is it possible to mourn the loss of someone you never actually had in the first place? Because I know I'll miss these feelings when it's all said and done.

"Of course, sir."

The waiter nods and walks away only to return with the wine a moment later.

"Just to let you know, we do have a couples special this evening. A starter salad, with an entree of your choice of salmon with vegetables, baked chicken with seasoned orzo, or porterhouse steak with a baked potato. Finishing off with our famous chocolate strawberry cheesecake. Are you ready to order now or would you like a few moments?"

Daniel eyes me like he's waiting for me to make the call.

"I'm good with the special if you are," I say before sipping my wine.

"Sounds fine to me. I'll do the baked chicken with orzo," he says to the waiter.

The waiter turns to me.

Normally on a date, I'd try to be the classy woman who got fish, but this is Daniel and it's not real. "I'll do the porterhouse and potato please."

Daniel raises his eyebrows at me in what I think is surprise. I love a good steak but normally only cook them for myself at the cottage. I always try to keep up appearances in public, but I'm not here to impress anyone tonight. I'm only here to *play pretend*. . . . Maybe if I tell myself that over and over again, it will bother me less. At the very least, it might keep my heart in check.

"Certainly, mam." The waiter smiles at me and then vanishes.

Fuck, I'm going to need more wine to get through this evening, because the longer this goes on, the more my anxiety grows. This was so stupid. Why did I have to open my damn mouth! I should have just been a big girl and told Mark the truth.

I watch the pianist play a soft, lovely jazz melody, doing my best not to meet Daniel's gaze. How can I go back to normal after this? Tonight is fantasy come to life, and how will I cope with the loss of it tomorrow? How will I see him every day knowing I'll never have any of this again?

"Rachel . . ." His voice is soft and laced with a concern that I don't recognize. Daniel is gruff and professional, and this is a different side of him.

Turning to look at him, I finally meet his gaze.

"I can take you home if this is too much."

Instinctively, I reach across the table and take hold of his hand. I need to touch him, to let him know I'm in this. And maybe the move was a little selfish, too. I wanted to feel him. His hand in mine instantly brought some peace to the storm in my brain. I don't think he has a single clue about the effect he has on me.

"No, I want to be here with you. This is just new and different for me, and I'm not quite sure what to do with myself." The confession feels vulnerable, and I don't like it, but it's so easy at the same time. He squeezes my hand gently, reassuringly almost, and we release our hold of each other.

"Oh, fake dating is new to you? I didn't realize, my bad," he jokes, and we both laugh, easing some of the awkwardness of the evening.

"So, tell me. Why didn't you have an *actual* date this evening?" I ask in a teasing way, but his eyebrows furrow together. I'm no idiot; I know he's single and almost forty for a reason. But as usual, I ask inappropriate questions.

He takes a sip of wine and then clears his throat. "I went into the Special Forces straight out of high school and from there joined the bodyguard industry. Most women have an issue with my need for control, and after a while I gave up on the notion of a family." He states it all like he's reciting a résumé, with a complete lack of emotion.

His words make my heart ache for him. "Daniel, I don't know anyone more deserving of a family than you."

He nods and clears his throat. "Now, my turn. Why don't *you* ever really date?"

I shift in my seat, uncomfortable with the question, but I had just put him in the hotseat, so I owe him an answer.

"Well, I don't have much experience with men, and with my father's line of work, I've seen the worst side of people. I guess I've been waiting for a man to want me for me and not just the power I come with as an heiress. But Daniel, just so you know, I like that you take control. I never have to worry with you by my side."

He smiles at me and my chest blooms with warmth.

There is an intimacy to the conversation; we're laying our souls bare to one another and it's as easy as looking at the stars and seeing them sparkle. I lack experience, but I've never connected with someone like this before, and it's both beautiful and terrifying.

Daniel leans in slightly. "Baby girl, you are so much more than an heiress to me."

And I feel his words deep in my soul. I watch as he lets out a shaky breath and wets his bottom lip. Is he going to break every rule and kiss me? He wouldn't. He couldn't possibly reciprocate my feelings. Still, though, there's a current. A gravity that's calling me to him.

Kiss me, Daniel. Show me that you care for me as I

do you and the rest of the world be damned. I'd never say the words out loud, but if he reads me as well as I know he does, he will see the words in my eyes.

He reaches up and cups my neck in his hand, drawing me closer to him. I stare into his eyes, and I see it. The desire, the war he's been through, and the pain he still faces.

"I see you, Daniel," I whisper.

"And I see all of you."

He leans over, mere inches from my lips, when someone clears their throat next to us.

We are ripped from the moment.

Daniel releases me immediately and adjusts his shirt as he sits back.

"I apologize for interrupting, but we are here with your food." The waiter smiles at us, and I don't know if I should curse the waiter or thank him. Because if I would've kissed Daniel, there would have been no saving my heart.

This is fake, and it will be over in only an hour or two. I plan to make the most of it, but I need to remember my place before things go too far and I can't get back pieces of my heart. I've already messed up enough by forcing Daniel into this situation. I can't keep making things worse for him.

CHAPTER 6

DANIEL

BOUNDARIES. FUCK, I NEED TO keep boundaries and follow my own damn rules. That was too close. If the waiter hadn't come back, I would've kissed her. For the first time, it felt like a person could see the things I keep hidden—could see my soul—and every fiber of me screamed to forget everything else, but I can't cross that line and potentially ruin my career for a girl who is fifteen years younger than me.

I've been with my fair share of women. Hell, in the military, we call them walking mattresses because of how often we'd have them on their backs. But Rachel is something else. She is breaking through every brick and stone I've fortified my walls with, and I didn't even know it was happening until it was too late. How did this fake date transform into feeling like a real one so quickly?

We make small talk and laugh through most of dinner. There is a lightness to her that has her basically glowing, and I already know that after this goes back to a professional relationship, I'll be finding ways to see it again. For the first time since I started guarding her three years ago, she looks carefree in a public setting. Usually, out in this world, she is an heiress and conducts herself as such, but tonight she is just Rachel. God, is it breathtaking, and I'm honored I get to witness it.

The waiter returns after our meal with a large slice of cheesecake and a fork on each side of the plate. The dessert is beautiful to look at with its chocolate crust, light pink filling, and a thick drizzle of chocolate and slices of strawberries on top.

Rachel is almost bouncing in anticipation of it. She has always had an insatiable sweet tooth, and she reminds me of a kid at a birthday party dying for that first bite. She is so cute to watch.

She bites her bottom lip, suppressing a smile, and her eyes are alight with joy as she watches the waiter intently, just waiting for him to set it before us. Warmth spreads throughout my chest, and a smile of my own appears. I know I won't get much of that dessert, but I'll gladly sacrifice it just to watch her devour it.

"Oh my God! It looks incredible!" She beams at the waiter, and he smiles at her politely.

"Enjoy." And he, once again, disappears.

"I get the first bite," I tease while stabbing into its soft texture.

She scowls at me the same way a five-year-old would, and I'm doing everything I can not to laugh at her pinched lips and furrowed brows.

"That's not fair!" she pouts.

"Of course it is. If I don't take a bite now, I may not get any." I take my bite and the strawberry sweetness blooms on my tongue, followed by a hit of chocolate that is just enough to complement rather than over-power.

She shrugs and her smile returns while she picks up her fork. "Well, I guess that's a valid argument."

"Wait. Someone needs to document this. Did you just admit defeat?" I lean forward and she rolls her eyes, digging into the dessert.

"I would never do such a thing. Just admitting that your argument at least has a legitimate claim."

I shake my head and laugh, leaning back in the booth.

She takes her bite slowly, wrapping her red lips around the fork, and I watch her way more intently than is considered appropriate.

Her eyes flutter closed, and she lets out a soft moan. I suck in a breath, and the sound goes straight to my dick as fire fills my veins. Thoughts of her making those noises by my doing fill my mind, and images of all the ways I could defile her flash before my eyes. I'm paralyzed by watching her every move while she enjoys the dessert. Bite after bite, my dick grows harder, because those lips, those noises. She could be on her knees before me and those lush lips could be around my throbbing cock. I could draw those noises from her with my tongue between her thighs. . . . I feel like a damn teenager all over again, fit to burst just from the idea of touching her.

"Oh shit, I'm sorry! I didn't even notice till now you only had the one bite! You want the rest?" she asks, concerned, and it's exactly what I needed to rip my mind out of the trance I was in.

I meet her gaze, and I can see the disappointment in her eyes at the idea of giving up the sweet to me. It's a small gesture, but it unlocks something inside that I haven't felt in so long. I'm always the one to give up things, sacrifice for others. Hell, my entire career is being willing to die in someone else's place. But *she* is willing to sacrifice something she loves for *me*.

"No, baby girl. You enjoy it."

She doesn't waste time arguing and goes back to finish off the dessert. I watch her take the final bite, and her eyes flutter again as she savors it all. For a moment, I wonder whether she will run her finger over the plate to get the last of the chocolate. God, what a sight that would be, watching her suck her fingers clean. I would probably blow my load.

Thankfully she doesn't, and right on cue, the waiter arrives, allowing me to pay. He returns with my card and a few small chocolates, and I have to flood my brain with thoughts of dead bodies, shooting guns, and the most unsexy things I can think of, because when I stand, I can't have my cock hard as iron and at attention.

"Would you mind taking a photo of us in front of the fireplace quick?" Rachel asks and extends her phone to him.

"Of course, Miss." He takes it from her, and she stands, waiting for me to join her.

Great. Picture time, and I'm not sure if that photo will also show how desperate I have become for this woman.

I stand and offer Rachel my elbow, like a gentleman would. She takes it, and the touch sends a lightning bolt through me. We walk to stand in front of the stone fireplace, side by side, and I tuck her into me as she places a hand on my chest. Her touch is gentle and soft, and I wish I never had to let her go. She stares at the waiter, but my eyes are only on her. They're only ever on her. I've hidden and suppressed my feelings for her for years, and tonight I think my protective shelter was just blown wide open. I never want to let this woman go.

"All set," he says, handing her back the phone. "And you two make a lovely couple. It's not often we have guests with such obvious chemistry." He smiles at us and walks away, leaving us with his words hanging in the air.

Obvious chemistry. It's my job to know her forward, backward, and upside down. But my nerves spike because I think he was referring to the gravitational pull that has been encompassing us all evening.

CHAPTER 7

RACHEL

OUR NIGHT IS COMING TO a close. We have the evidence we need, and I got spoiled on a date. I should feel elated after this evening, but as I ride next to Daniel in the front seat of his SUV, my heart feels heavy and burdened.

This is what it must have been like for Cinderella when she went to the ball. She had the best night of her life with her Prince Charming, only for the clock to strike midnight and have to leave it all behind. Of course, in her story, the glass slipper was left, and she got her happily-ever-after. In my story, there will only be longing for what could never be and maybe a date with a rom-com movie and a pint of ice cream. I'm sure someday I'll find love, but I know I'll always wonder if Daniel could have been my true Prince Charming.

The drive is quiet, but Daniel's hand has enveloped mine since walking out of the restaurant. I savor the feel of his hand on mine, knowing if I ever hold his hand again, it will be for an urgent need. His rough, calloused hands are a contrast to mine being small and soft. His tell a story of a fighter and the battles he has faced. I've seen how fierce he can be. A lump forms in my throat as I realize the only time I've seen this man soft or gentle is when he's dealing with me.

Having pulled up to my cottage, he climbs down from the driver's seat. My eyes track his every move, swooning over every inch of him tonight. I catalogue each stride and flex of his muscles so they will forever live in my memories. He opens the passenger door for me, and I climb out, knowing that in just a few moments, this will become nothing more than the night of pretend it was supposed to be.

He places a hand on my lower back and walks with me to my front door. How will I be able to face him sitting at my table tomorrow or taking me to classes later this week? The whole point of this was so nothing would change, but for me, everything has. My heart has split open wide, and I'm nothing more than a walking ball of emotion.

Reaching the door, I turn to him. "Thank you for a wonderful evening."

His hand moves to my waist and butterflies fill my belly.

"It was my pleasure." His tone is soft and husky. It may be the sexiest sound I've ever heard. Heat floods my core, and the look in his soft eyes tells me he feels this, too.

This shift between us.

There's no going back to the ignored feelings and professional relationship we shared. Maybe that's why I feel bold. I don't want to let go without even trying.

"Daniel . . ." My voice shakes with the nervousness I feel. I will never recover if he rejects me. "Will you kiss me, please?"

His eyes examine mine as he wages what appears to be an internal war. He runs his hand over his beard and his eyes leave mine for a moment, then come back, fire in them.

"Fuck it," he whispers, and his other hand cups my neck and I tip my chin as his thick, pillow-soft lips kiss me, slowly and tenderly.

Something clicks into place in this moment. A knowing that this is who I am meant to be with. I'm not sure if I believe in soulmates, but whatever is drawing Daniel and me together is far greater than just lust and desire.

I press into his kiss, making it deeper as I lace my fingers into his hair. He groans against my lips, and his tongue claims my mouth, the taste of wine and strawberries still lingering.

He presses me to the door and fire ignites inside me as his hard appendage presses into my pelvis. I've never felt this overwhelming need to be with someone so bad in my life. I want to claim him. No, I want to be claimed by him.

After a moment, he pulls his lips from mine, both of our chests heaving.

"I should go, Rachel. I'm your bodyguard and you're too young for me." His eyebrows furrow together.

I pull my hand from his hair and rest it gently on his cheek. "If you want to leave, I won't try and stop you, because you're right. But if you want this and feel what I feel, then bring me into the cottage and take care of me, Daniel."

His eyes stare into mine with the same longing I feel, but the question is, will he brave enough to act on it?

"What are you doing to me, sweetheart?" he asks before pulling me off the door, turning the knob, leading me inside.

CHAPTER 8

DANIEL

THERE HAVE BEEN MOMENTS IN my life where I know no matter what I choose, it will change everything. Where I must decide to be brave and walk into the unknown or stay still and pray that what I never pursued doesn't become a regret.

On the porch with Rachel was one of those moments, and I knew that if I had chosen to leave, I would have regretted it until the day I died.

As soon as we're both through the door, I lock it behind us. She looks like a god damn goddess, and somehow, she wants me. She saunters to her bedroom, and my cock aches with anticipation of what's coming. I follow close behind her, already desperate to touch her once more.

She stops in the middle of the room, and I'm not playing follow the leader any longer. I'm in charge of this now.

I walk to her and tip her chin so her eyes lock with mine. "I'm going to kiss you again, and if at any point you want this to stop, just say the word. I'll never hurt you, sweetheart. Not unless you want me to." Her breathing hitches slightly, and pride blooms inside me at the sound.

She nods at me, her cheeks flushing a bright pink that travels down her neck. I don't miss a beat, and I claim her mouth once more. The sweetness of the chocolate and wine still lingers. She is so damn intoxicating, like my own personal drug that I will never get enough of and now will forever crave.

The kiss is hot and erotic as our mouths and tongues dance together like we're starved. My hands travel down her back, to her plump, round ass, and her moans fill my mouth as she pushes into my touch. Her hands start to scratch at my back, and I need to feel her, to have more of her. I pick her up and she instantly wraps her legs around me, never breaking our kiss.

I walk us to the bed and lay her down gently while I sit up between her legs. Her eyes track every single one of my movements as I unbutton my shirt and remove it. They travel over me, and I smirk at her as she starts to squirm.

"Like what you see?"

"God, yes." She is absolutely breathless with need. Need for me.

I touch her bare thighs and start feeling my way up to her panties as her breathing picks up with a nervous energy.

I remove my hands from her. "We can stop if you don't want this, Rachel." My dick may fall off from the denial, but I will stop. I meant it when I said I would never hurt her.

"Please don't stop. I just . . . I've never . . ." she fumbles with her words.

"You've never had a man eat your pussy before?" I ask, trying to help.

She shakes her head at me. "I've never had any of it before."

My eyebrows furrow, and I stare at her, trying to piece together what she's saying. It takes me longer than it should to register what she's just told me, but something deep and primal awakens in me when I figure it out. She has never had these experiences before, and I get to be the man to claim her.

"You're a virgin."

"Yes. I'm sorry I didn't tell you sooner. It's just a little embarrassing to be twenty-two and have never had these experiences." Her cheeks redden, but she has no need to be embarrassed.

I climb over her and cup her cheek. "I'm honored to be your first." I allow my words to settle over her and hope my eyes convey to her all the deep feelings I hold in those words. She nods, smiling at me softly, and I know she's okay.

I sit up again and pick up where I left off: running my fingers over her thighs, up her dress, over her full, soft tits, and then I pull her dress up and off her.

She stares at me with hooded eyes as I take in the sight of her milky skin and her red lace bra and panties. I don't think I have ever seen a more perfect woman.

"Like what you see?" she teases nervously, parroting my earlier choice of words.

"Yeah, Rachel. I really do," I growl, claiming her with a kiss full of hungry need. My hands explore her abdomen and tits while her body arches into my touch. Moving from her lips, I suck and kiss her neck. She tilts her head, creating just the right angle.

I pull her up to my chest and remove her bra. My hand envelopes one breast, and I tease her pebbled nipple into a perfect peak.

"Your tits are fucking flawless, sweetheart."

She arches her chest up, begging me for more.

I kiss and suck a trail down her delicate skin until I finally reach her nipple and take it into my mouth while kneading her other side.

She moans and starts running her finger through my hair, stoking the need I have for her. I want her so damn bad, it's getting painful, but I love playing with her. She is so damn perfect, and she doesn't even realize it.

I move to the other side and grant it equal attention. "Daniel, please. More please," she whimpers, pressing her thighs together.

My cock is weeping for her, but this isn't about me tonight. This is about treating her like the queen she is.

Smiling against her skin, I leave her tits and kiss down her abdomen until I reach the apex of her thighs. "Do you think you'll taste as good as you smell, sweetheart?"

She moans softly at my words and lets her legs fall wide for me.

It's the only invitation I need, and I instantly run my tongue from her entrance to her swollen clit. She cries out and lurches up. So, I place a hand on her abdomen to hold her still as I feast on her perfect pussy. I swirl my tongue over her clit and insert a finger into her tight, wet entrance.

"Ah, oh fuck . . ." she mewls, and I add a second finger, placing pressure onto her upper wall right into the perfect spot. Her sweet, pleasure-filled cries get louder, and her thighs start to quake.

"That's it. Come for me." My command sends her over the precipice as her orgasm courses through her.

"Ah . . . oh god . . . Daniel!" she cries out, and I don't think I've heard my name sound so beautifully before.

"You are so gorgeous when you come, sweetheart." I wipe my face and smile at her. "That might just be my new favorite meal."

She bites her bottom lip, and I stand from the bed, removing my pants. Her eyes instantly land on my cock, and I pull a condom from my wallet, rolling it down myself before returning to the bed.

I climb over her, and her breathing picks up with the same nervous energy from before.

"It's okay if you want to stop, just say the word." Brushing my knuckles over her cheek, I search her eyes for any regret, but I can't find any.

"I want you, Daniel, all of you."

I nod at her words.

"Okay, this is the worst part. The rest will feel good. I promise, I will make this feel good for you." I line myself up to her entrance.

"Fuck me, please, Daniel," she whimpers.

I kiss her deeply as I thrust myself inside her tight, wet center.

She cries out, and I still myself, letting her adjust to me, but fuck is it hard. She is so tight; I feel ready to bust already.

I kiss her gently, savoring the feel of her lips on mine, and wait for her to let me know she's ready. It doesn't take long for her to start rocking her hips against me.

I follow her lead and begin pumping into her. Her fingernails scrape along my back and, fuck, it's driving me wild. She's mine now. This night, this moment, is binding her to me.

Her legs start to quiver around me, and her pussy

starts to flutter. She's close, and so am I. Two more thrusts and I spill into her.

My soul may have left my body with how hard I come.

She's pushed over the edge with me. "Daniel," she moans while her pussy milks my cock for every last drop. The sound of my name on her lips while she falls apart is something that will be burned into my mind until the day I die.

We lie together, relishing the feel of each other before I remove myself from her and she winces slightly.

"I wasn't too rough, was I?" I ask, concerned, as I brush a hair from her face, but her eyes sparkle at me, something deep within shining through.

"No, you were perfect. I wouldn't have wanted it any different." Her soft smile makes my heart swell. She's perfect. Everything I wanted and never knew I needed.

Standing from the bed, I walk to her bathroom. I remove the condom and dispose of it in the trash. I turn to her large soaking tub and start the warm water. I find the Epsom salts in the sink cabinet. After adding a generous amount, I put it away and walk back to her room to find her curled up and snuggling her pillow. She is exhausted, but I promised I would always take care of her, and this is part of that.

"Come here." I reach down and cradle her body to my chest and she rests her head on my shoulder.

"What are you doing?" She snickers but snuggles into me.

"Taking care of you," I whisper against her forehead as I place a soft kiss on it. We enter the bathroom, and I gently lower her into the tub. A satisfied moan escapes her as the warmth wraps around her.

I've never been a bath man, but the idea of leaving her in it alone is like a punch to the gut, so I slide in behind her.

She leans back into my chest, and I wrap my arms around her, a little afraid that she'll float away or something.

"This whole night has been a dream, Daniel. Thank you for seeing all of me and always knowing what I need. I can't imagine my first time being any more perfect. You're better than I could have ever dreamed, Wolf."

Wolf. That is a nickname I rarely hear anymore. It was a nickname given to me because I'm a loner. I never settled down with a partner, I always prefer to work alone, and my friend group is stupid small. But the thing about wolves is they are fiercely loyal, and they mate for life. I don't think she's calling me a loner, but she's referring to something much deeper with that name.

"Rest now, sweetheart, just let me take care of you."

CHAPTER 9

RACHEL

I WAKE UP TO THE early morning sun shining through my bedroom curtains, and my bed is empty beside me. My chest pangs at the idea he could be gone, or that it was just some wild dream, but the scents of fresh coffee and bacon is floating in from the kitchen. Instantly the sick feeling is replaced with fire in my chest. My heart feels fit to burst after last night, and there's a small ache between my legs to remind me just how special it truly was.

The way his gentle hands touched me, the way his mouth felt on mine, the way he filled me perfectly . . . It was better than I had ever imagined possible. He cared so deeply for me last night, and he stayed over, never leaving my side.

He's stayed overnight before on the couch when it

was necessary for the job, but he has never cared for me so tenderly. Having him in my bed is better than I ever thought possible.

I climb from my bed and wrap my naked body in Daniel's button-up shirt and head to the kitchen. Daniel is only wearing his boxer briefs as he works at the stove, and I'm in no hurry to alert him to my presence. I swear I could stare at that perfectly sculpted ass forever, and last night I got a full view of those tattoos. On his left arm is only a half sleeve covering his forearm, but on the right side is a full sleeve that comes up over his chest and covers the one shoulder down over his back shoulder blade. I want to inspect each one. Take my time to admire every intricate design.

He turns to the coffee pot, and I'm caught red-handed ogling him. But I don't care. After last night, I'll ogle whenever I damn well please.

"Good morning." I smile and walk up behind him so I can wrap my arms around him.

"Good morning. How'd you sleep?"

"Wonderfully, you?"

He spins to hold me to his front, cupping my ass with his firm hands. "Best sleep of my life." His voice is raw and gruff.

He leans down to kiss me, softly invading my mouth, and my core goes molten, but longing filling my heart. We're in a blissful bubble right now, and I'm scared of what happens when it pops.

He pulls away from me to remove the bacon from the stove and shut off the burner. "Are you hungry? I planned to wake you with breakfast, but you beat me to it." He smiles.

"Sure." I nod. He reaches over, grabs a cup of coffee, and sets it down in front of me. "But can we talk about what happens after this?" I ask as the worry of having to say goodbye grows. I just can't bear to have the unknown sitting on my shoulders anymore. I have to rip off the band-aid.

He sighs and brushes his hand through his hair. I take a sip of my coffee and my heart cracks a little, because he's made it just the way I like it. They say without pain you will never know love, and even though saying goodbye is going to obliterate me, I still would have rather had him for one night than not all.

I wrap my arms around myself, trying to brace for the blow to come.

"I knew this conversation was coming," he mutters.

I shove down the lump forming in my throat. I will not cry in front of him. I'm stronger than that. I knew this was a temporary thing coming into it, and I have no regrets . . . at least not yet.

"Rachel, I know this was supposed to be one night, and I'll leave and pretend like nothing happened if that's what you want, baby girl." He takes my chin in his thumb, forcing me to meet his eyes. "But *I* don't want to. I want to take you on a real date and sleep in your bed." His eyes burn with love beneath the surface and my chest swells. "I want to break the number one rule and date my client. I want to show you love and cherish every moment with you if you'll let me."

Is it possible for a human heart to combust with joy and adoration for someone? If yes, then call me an ambulance, because I'm goner. I kiss him hard, lacing my fingers through his hair.

Pulling back, I rest my forehead against his. "Yes, Wolf. I want this with you. I want to see if we mate for life."

"Might be a short life, baby girl. Your dad might kill me," he teases as he walks to the counter, grabbing the plate of bacon and a bowl of scrambled eggs.

He heads to my small dining table and sets down the food. Normally, I would scold myself for still having my textbooks on the living room floor, but right now I'm grateful, because if they weren't out there, they'd be in here. I take a seat and start fixing my plate. He watches me for a moment with a slight smirk before following suit and I feel my cheeks start to redden. I hope he was just admiring me, and I didn't do something stupid.

"So, I like to keep things out in the open. What do you think about heading to the main house and speaking to your dad about us after breakfast?"

I stop chewing mid-bite. I can't blame him for wanting to be upfront with everything, but I didn't plan for that. I know Dad won't react well, but Daniel's right, and hopefully Dad won't kill him.

"Umm, yeah, if that's what you want to do."

He smiles and nods as he takes a bite of his food. Is he actually looking forward to my dad possibly freaking out?

Images and ideas of how this meeting may go start to flood my brain. This could be *bad*. He could yell, he could break Daniel's hand—hell, he could string him up in the basement and skin him alive with a hot knife so he wouldn't bleed out.

Shaking all of it from my head, I decide to focus on something beautiful and sweet instead and turn my attention to the roses on the dining room table.

I gesture to the flowers. "Thank you for the pre-date roses, by the way. I know they were part of the act, but I like them all the same."

He puts his fork down and tilts his head slightly to the side, his eyebrows pinched. "I never sent you or left you these flowers."

"What do you mean? The card said, 'Counting the minutes until I hold you in my arms,' and it was signed 'Your Special Someone.'"

Daniel's jaw ticks slightly and he pulls out his phone.

"What are you doing?"

"I'm messaging Rob and letting him know to meet us at the main house in ten minutes. I never sent you those flowers, and we need to find out right now who did."

And just like that, our blissful bubble pops, just

not the way I thought it would. Daniel stands, takes his plate to the kitchen, and then heads to the bedroom. I watch as he marches around like this is a serious threat when I'd bet it's most likely a joke someone has played.

When I was abducted, there was no warning. I was shopping, and when I went out to my car, a black van stopped and shoved me in. No one saw it coming. Growing up, I learned most games are played in the shadows and then the attack comes when it's unexpected. A real threat wouldn't have left a warning.

"Rachel, get dressed. Now." His voice is clipped as he emerges from the bedroom in his pants from last night.

"Fine, but I think you're being a bit excessive here," I state as I rise from the table and walk past him to my room.

"Sweetheart, when it comes to your safety, you haven't begun to see excessive." His voice is threateningly low. He's so concerned about those damn flowers and mysterious note.

I should've just thrown them in the trash.

CHAPTER 10
DANIEL

MY MIND JUMPS INSTANTLY TO Peter, the new intern at the Mirage Tower. There were a few stills in the recon photos of him picking up red roses but nothing on a romantic relationship. I thought it was odd but not concerning enough to worry about until now. The roses would also link him to the Crimson Bears, which we have been suspicious of anyway since he started at the Tower. There have been rumors that roses might be the Bears' new calling card, but nothing concrete enough to know for sure yet.

"There. Happy?" Rachel asks, throwing my shirt at me and gesturing to her T-shirt and jeans. I would love to take a moment to admire the curve of her ass in them, then slowly pull them off them and sink my teeth into the soft skin beneath. *Fuck*, this is why dating clients is bad. She is a distraction. I slide on my soiled shirt and roll my shoulders.

"Yes. Let's go." It comes out harsher than I intend it to, but I have too many emotions running through me right now to express anything other than anger.

"Whatever, Daniel." She shoves past me and whips the door open, marching her sassy little ass toward the main house.

I'm irritated that she's not taking this seriously. She's already been abducted once, and I have no intention of having it happen again. I would be a fucking felon because I would murder anyone who laid a hand on her.

Rachel enters through the large, oak door of the main house before I even make it to the white, concrete porch. The Hudson Estate home is exactly what you would expect for a family with old money: the house is massive and way bigger than one family should ever need.

I step up on to the porch and Rob swings the front door open, steps out, and shuts it behind him. His face is downcast, his shoulders slumped and his hands in his pockets. My stomach sours at the sight. Something more is going on here, and I need to get to Rachel now.

I try walking around him, but his hand catches my arm. "Daniel, we have been associates for a long time now." For looking upset, his tone is eerily calm. "Is there anything you want to tell me before we walk in there?"

I turn to face him now, feeling my brows furrowed

in confusion. "What the hell are you talking about? We're here about the Crimson Bears. Why are you questioning me like this?"

"Daniel, tell me now and I might be able to help you," he whispers and looks around for others who may be watching.

"I don't need help. I need to protect Rachel," I say with finality and yank open the front door.

Rob doesn't speak, only follows close behind as I walk the main hallway to Mr. Hudson's office. I knock, then open the door to reveal Rachel sitting in a fluffy brown chair and her father leaning his backside against his desk with his arms crossed over his chest.

"Good, you've joined us. Daniel take a seat," he commands as he rubs his hand over his salt-and-peppered mustache and goatee.

I take a step forward. "Sir, we have a situation that needs—"

"I said sit." He pushes off his desk and speaks with his full authority. This is not the time to challenge him.

I take my seat next to Rachel, and Mr. Hudson adjusts his gray suit jacket and returns to his spot. I want to look at Rachel, make sure she's okay and reassure her, but I don't dare.

We all sit in silence a long moment as my boss's deathly gaze rakes over me. He knows or suspects something, but this needs to wait. I need to let them know of the real threat that looms.

"I received a note this morning with an interesting picture inside. Would you two like to tell me anything?"

Out of the corner of my eye, I see Rachel shift uncomfortably.

"Yes, sir, Rachel has received a set of roses to her porch with an anonymous note. I believe—"

Mr. Hudson moves in front of me and crouches so he's eye level with me. A new fury burns in his eyes, and I seem to be the target of his rage.

"That's not what I want to hear right now!" he booms. "I'm talking about the fact that a member of my staff took my daughter on a date and appears to have spent the night with her!" He gestures at my clothes.

I stare back at him, refusing to back down or show remorse. I will not feel bad for my actions with Rachel.

"Daddy, I can explain," Rachel's sweet voice chimes in, but Mr. Hudson holds up his hand to silence her. He stands and moves to his desk and lifts a photo showing Rachel and me sharing dessert at Pontera's.

A heavy feeling settles in my gut, as any doubt that I was overreacting about the roses disappears. I sit forward in my seat, anxious to look at the photo and read the note that arrived with it.

"Sir, I understand that you're upset I got involved with your daughter, but there's something more pressing."

"More pressing than having one of my bodyguards betray my trust and defile my daughter?" His voice has turned threateningly low, and I know if I'm not careful, he'll tell Rob to take me to the basement. Down there, death becomes a mercy.

"Only because it threatens her safety and possibly her life."

He glances at his daughter, who looks ready to cry with pink cheeks and sad eyes. My heart pangs, and I want only to wrap her in my arms.

"I'm listening," he grumbles and sits in his desk chair.

"Yesterday morning, I sent a report on Peter Malvo." I stand from my seat and pause to make sure it's okay. "He's the new intern at the Tower. We have multiple images of him purchasing roses, but we have nothing on what he did with them, and he has a felony stalking charge. His employment at the Tower could tie him to the Crimson Bears and could potentially make the roses a warning of an attack from them."

He sighs and tosses the photo and note to me. Then he gestures for Rob to step out from the corner he was standing in.

"This is more important than you and my daughter, but just know that conversation is not over, Daniel."

I nod. "I understand, sir."

"Rachel, please head to the kitchen and get some coffee going for us," Mr. Hudson says, and she makes no attempt to argue. She just stands and leaves us, swatting away a stray tear.

I watch as she shuts the door behind her, and I feel this deep need to be beside her. If they got into this estate, how can I trust she's safe anywhere?

"Now, I received this note and photo sometime overnight. It was on the front step, which means that if this is connected to the roses, whoever is behind this has gotten into this estate twice."

I lift the note and read it. *You chose wrong. Your bodyguard is a liar.*

You chose wrong. What choice did he make, and what does it have to do with me?

"What choice?" I ask, glancing between Rob and Mr. Hudson.

"That is the big question, isn't it? I'm assuming it has to do with you dating my daughter."

Rob steps forward. "Sir, I have a theory. What if instead of trying to overthrow us, maybe the Bears intend to have Peter marry Rachel, and then kill off you and Simon to take over since she would be the only remaining heir?"

Every fiber of me screams, and I clench my fists at the idea that this could be their intention. No one will touch my girl and live to breathe another day.

"It's a solid theory. Rob, go dig deeper into this Peter Malvo, but I also want to explore other theories. Daniel, you will look into everyone denied your bodyguard position. Answers may be in there since *I chose wrong.* You also will continue guarding my daughter.

Whoever this is, I don't want them to think their goal has been accomplished by eliminating you."

He moves to the filing cabinet below his desk and begins stacking files on his desk.

"Thank you, sir. I'll keep her safe." It's a promise.

"You better. Now both of you get to work and get the hell out of my office. I need to call my son and make sure he's not having any issues in his negotiations with the Cartel. We don't need any additional problems right now."

I nod and scoop up the stack of files, then quickly head to the kitchen to find my girl. She's just pouring a cup of coffee when I walk in.

"Hey, baby girl, we're done, and I just got flooded with work." I hold up the stack of files. "Care to head back to the cottage and help me?"

"Sure. I can do that." Her voice is still soft, and she won't make eye contact. My heart is splitting at the sight, but I can't help her. Not here. I watch as she scurries quietly to her dad's office with his cup. She's back a moment later.

"Let's go, baby girl," I say softly, gesturing for her to lead the way.

She moves slowly, all the earlier fight gone, and I follow her out the door and across the property to the small cottage without a single word spoken between us.

CHAPTER 11

RACHEL

THIS ISN'T A PRANK OR some joke. I'm actually under attack again, and on top of that, my dad is *furious* with Daniel. I've made such a damn mess of everything.

I walk through my front door, and I'm greeted with the comforts of home. My chest aches and tears threaten my eyes. I'm not safe, and I'm going to lose Daniel. Dad's never going to allow us to be together after all this.

"So, how long until you leave?" I'm not prepared for the answer, but I'd rather get all the heartache out of the way.

Daniel sets the files down on the dining room table and wraps his arms around me, pulling me to his firm chest. I melt into his embrace and savor his warmth and scent. I allow a sense of peace to fill me, if only for this short moment.

"I'm not. Your dad still has me guarding you. I won't be leaving your side until this is taken care of."

"And after that?" I can't help the cynicism I feel over this situation.

"I'm not sure what's going to happen with your dad, but I waited a long time to hold you in my arms and I'll be damned if I let you go without a fight." He squeezes me a little tighter and kisses my forehead.

Warmth bubbles in my chest, and I can't hold in the soft smile that forms on my face.

"Sweetheart, let's just enjoy right now and let the future worry about itself."

I nod against him. He's right. We can enjoy today. I'll make the most of whatever time we have left. We have been mere feet apart for years, both unknowingly longing for one another. I want to cherish every moment with him.

I turn my face up to his and kiss his lips, enjoying the softness of them. I'll never tire of kissing him.

"So, files or lunch?" I ask with an uptick to my voice. "I'll cook since you did breakfast."

"Lunch sounds great. I'll get started on the files while you get to work." He smiles down at me, and the moment almost feels as normal as this morning's— before the chaos began.

He releases me and I turn to head to the kitchen. As

I walk away, Daniel smacks my ass with a loud clap, and I yelp.

"What was that for?" I face him with fake outrage.

"Just enjoying what's mine." He shrugs nonchalantly.

I laugh and then turn back to the kitchen.

The rest of the day passes quickly. We enjoy our lunch and then review files in which we find nothing of interest. There's still a stack left, but my brain is fried, and I just want to enjoy my man. Daniel had to skip poker night with the guys for the work before us, so a nice evening would do him good, too, I think.

"Can we put this away and just do wine and a movie?"

"I really need to get through these tonight." He doesn't even bother looking up from the file he's currently reading through.

I stand from the table and walk to the kitchen. I pull down two wine glasses and grab the bottle of Moscato from the wine rack. The stems of the roses sticking out of the trash can catch my eye, and I let out a soft sigh before heading back to the never-ending stack of files.

"Wolf, look at me." I use my firmest tone, and his head shoots up. "We have been working all day, and I just want to enjoy the evening with you."

He stands from his seat, takes both glasses from my hand, and smiles at me softly. "Fine, one movie," he concedes, and I start to bounce with joy.

"Thank you!" I reach up and peck him on the lips quickly and then head toward the living room.

"When did the deer start telling the wolf what to do?" he teases, but I ignore him.

Flopping down on the couch, I grab the remote from the coffee table and flip through the streaming channels' movie options while Daniel sets down the glasses, takes the bottle, and starts to fill them. I settle on a good rom-com and snuggle into Daniel as I hit play.

"First you convince me to stop working, and now you have me watching a chick flick," he grumbles, and I only giggle. "Oh, the things I do for you, baby girl." He kisses my cheek, and I snuggle further into him, savoring the feel of his strong arms wrapping around me.

Half a bottle of wine later, the couple on the screen is finally realizing they can't live without each other, and I turn to look up at Daniel. He isn't looking at the television screen. He's staring back at me with a sweetness in his eyes that makes my heart skip a beat.

One date was all it took for us both to let our feelings and desires for one another out of the cages we'd locked them in for so long.

"You aren't watching the movie." It comes out almost like a whisper.

"I'd rather watch you, right here in my arms." He leans down and rests his forehead against mine, and all my interest in the movie evaporates.

I lean up, kissing him softly, as my hand finds the back of his neck. He lifts me and turns me so I straddle his lap. His hands find my hips, squeezing just enough, and I press my chest into his while our lips continue dancing together.

I pull back from him and stare into his gorgeous, green eyes. "It's been a long day, and I think I could use a shower."

"I think I can definitely help with that." His chest rumbles as he speaks, and he stands from the couch, taking me with him, my legs wrapped around him. He kisses me harder this time, his tongue invading my mouth as he walks us to the bathroom.

Heat floods my core and goosebumps cover my skin. I want to feel him. I want him to cherish me like his queen, and I want to savor everything about him. I run my hands over his back to the nape of his neck and push my fingers through his hair.

We enter the bathroom, and he kicks the door shut behind us. He sets me on the cool counter and my senses alight from the contrast between the heat I feel and the cold on the marble surface soaking through my clothes.

Daniel releases me from his hold. "Stay. Don't move a single inch, sweetheart." His voice is rough and commanding and makes me want to physically melt for this man.

He turns and starts the shower and removes his shirt, tossing it aside. Then he faces me as he undoes his belt and drops his pants and boxer briefs to the floor.

I press my thighs together as my sex throbs at the sight of him. My mouth parts as my breathing quickens. I need this man. How did I end up with such an incredible being to call mine? He steps to me, taking hold of my waist.

"Your turn now." He leans forward, kissing just below my earlobe as he starts to remove my jeans.

I pant with need and press into his touch. He steps back, and I lift my hips as he removes my jeans and panties. My bare skin hits the cool counter, and it only makes things more erotic.

He kneels in front of me and puts both legs over his shoulders. He runs a finger along my dripping folds.

"So, fucking beautiful . . . and all fucking mine." He growls and begins feasting on me.

"Oh, god," I whimper as he sucks my swollen clit into his mouth, then runs his tongue from my entrance back to it. He starts drawing delicious circles over it.

I moan as pure pleasure overtakes me, and my fingers find my way into his hair again. He pulls back and his eyes meet mine.

"Watch me, sweetheart. Watch me devour your beautiful cunt and enjoy the sight of me on my knees before you."

I damn near come at his words.

He returns to my needy sex, and I watch as he takes me. God, is it invigorating and intoxicating. My thighs start to tremble, and I pull him deeper to me as my climax builds higher and higher.

He slides two fingers into me. "That's it, come for me." He pumps in and out of me and sucks my clit into his mouth once more. He presses his tongue flat against it, then presses up harder with his fingers and I explode.

"Oh God, Daniel!"

He stands in front of me, wiping my cum from his face, a proud smile on his lips.

I plant my hands on the counter and try to steady my body as it trembles in aftershock.

His eyes drink me in as he steps forward, kissing me hard, and I taste myself on him. He lifts my shirt and removes it, along with my bra. It stokes the flames still burning in me.

"You look perfect when you come, sweetheart. And when my name falls from those trembling lips, I'm pretty sure angels weep at the hallelujah it is."

A breathy moan leaves me. "Daniel . . ."

He lifts me from the counter and brings us into the warm shower. The heat sears my cool skin, and I moan on the impact of the droplets.

He lowers me to stand, and I place a firm hand on his chest. He steps back, into the stream of water, and I drop to my knees in front of him.

"Rachel—"

"My turn now," I say, looking straight up at him. He nods and gathers my hair into his hands.

I take hold of his cock and run my tongue over the tip, tasting the salty sweetness of his precum. I slowly take him into my mouth and watch as he throws his head back and groans.

I take him deeper and start pumping up and down on him. Water pelts my hair and drips down my face, making it even more sensuous.

"That's it, baby girl. Just like that." His hungry voice fuels me, and I relax my throat, taking him all the way to the hilt.

"Fuck, you look so good taking all of me," he rasps, and I moan around him.

I pump up and down, tears springing to my eyes. I want to taste him like he has me. I want to be the best he has had and savor every drop of him.

"I'm going to come, baby girl. You ready for that?" His voice is hoarse, and I know he's holding back.

I press into him, gripping his wet thighs. I moan around him once more, letting him know I want it.

Two more pumps and he explodes. The saltiness blooms on my tongue. I swallow everything he gives me. I refuse to waste even a single drop of him. *Mine. He is mine.*

I stand with pride in my chest. He kisses me deep and hard, pressing me flat to the shower wall, and his hand cups my cheek.

He rests his forehead to mine. "You're so fucking perfect, baby girl."

"Hmmm." I smile and my chest warms instantly.

With this man, I'm not a striving doctor or feminist with big goals. I'm a submissive woman, and the idea of one day carrying a child of his has me ready to buckle at the knees.

"Now, let's get you cleaned up so I have a fresh canvas to dirty again later."

I laugh and smile as he pulls down my luffa and soap. "I'll hold you to that, Wolf."

CHAPTER 12

DANIEL

I PULL MYSELF FROM THE bed where Rachel was sleeping next to me. After the shower, we climbed into bed and she promptly fell asleep in my arms.

She's so peaceful and beautiful lying here with nothing but a sheet covering her, but work calls my name, and I need to finish those files tonight.

I cover her with the comforter so she doesn't get cold. I slide my pants on and head back to the table where work awaits. This is probably a pointless endeavor, but I need to be sure—and also show John Hudson that I can still properly prioritize even though I'm seeing his daughter.

The more I succeed here, the less likely he is to fire me or kill me.

I skim file after file and nothing of interest shows up. I had no idea that more than seventy people interviewed for this job, and somehow, I got it. I have a better understanding of why my dating Rachel is hitting Mr. Hudson so hard. I was supposed to be the best, and Mr. Hudson probably sees me as the wrong choice just like that note said.

I plop the second to last file down in front of me and glance at the clock on the wall. It's three in the morning. I sigh, recognizing that it will be a mostly sleepless night, but the lack of sleep is worth it to keep my girl safe.

Flopping the folder open, rage instantly hits me as soon as I see the photo and name. Mark Kirklan. That's what he meant in the garage when he talked about living in my shadow and getting the life he wants. He wanted my job. And then he wanted Rachel.

I read through the file with a fine-toothed comb, hoping to find anything useful, but I don't find anything I didn't already know. The most interesting thing about him was that he served as a Navy SEAL for four years before leaving and becoming a bodyguard for hire.

He doesn't strike me as a man who would target Rachel for personal gain, but then again, he spent years serving our country and then years trying to build a business. For a thirty-year-old man, he doesn't have much to show for it.

His file will be joining me at tomorrow morning's, or more like today's, debrief with Mr. Hudson and

Rob. I close the folder and quickly review the last one before dragging my body back to Rachel's bed. She's exactly how I left her, and my heart swells at the sight. I slide in next to her and wrap her into my arms, and she instantly cuddles to me. I have to be up in a little over three hours, but all I want to do is savor the feel of her until dawn.

My alarm sounds on my phone and Rachel groans beside me. I'm not sure when I fell asleep, but I feel like it's been mere minutes. I shut off the alarm and sit up in the bed, trying to force my brain to come to life.

"I'm not coming," Rachel groans into her pillow.

Oh, how I want to force her to come with me simply because she said she isn't going to.

I lean over and place my hand on her hip, rubbing gently. "I think you have to."

"Ugh." She groans loud into the pillow and a smile forms on my face.

"Fine, I'll have mercy. Stay here and sleep, but don't leave the cottage without calling."

"Deal." Her voice is still muffled by the pillow, and then she wraps herself into a ball with the blanket.

I tap her hip gently, chuckling under my breath, and climb from the bed. It's too damn early for all of this, but the bad guys don't stop or take rest days so neither can I. Soon I'll be able to stay in bed all day with Rachel if I want to, or at least, I hope I will.

Once I'm dressed, I scoop up the folder and head

out the door. On the other side, I find Rob approaching the cottage with what looks like two coffees and a small duffle bag.

"What's all that?" I ask as he grows closer.

"Well, I figured you could use a suit since you've been staying here. So, I brought you one that was too big for me. It was just hanging in my closet."

He hands me the duffle, and I unzip it to reveal the clothing folded neatly inside.

"Thank you. I really appreciate it, Rob."

"No problem. The second coffee is for you, too. I assumed you were up all night working like I was."

"You assumed right. Thank you again." I take the coffee and sip the hot liquid. It's like the perfect fall morning in a cup. A good day always starts with a good cup of joe.

"I'll see you up there." He waves as he turns and heads toward the main house.

I duck back into the cottage and change into the suit as quickly as possible. I dash out the door, not bothering to pick up my discarded clothes, and head to the main house. As I enter, I note the silence of the house, and I make my way to Mr. Hudson's office, where we usually meet.

I slide the door open indand enter. Mr. Hudson is seated behind his desk. Rob stands to his right, and someone is seated in the chair in front of them. I walk past, not sparing a glance at the guest, and take my place on my boss's left.

Then I make eye contact with Peter Malvo. The tall, lean man is resting against the back of the chair with his one foot thrown over his other leg. He looks entirely bored. For an intern kid with a rose fetish, he sure does have one hell of an arrogant demeanor.

"Thank you for joining us, Daniel. We'll discuss your tardiness later." Mr. Hudson side-eyes me.

I internally grimace but being late and dressed appropriately is better than coming in here yet again in my date clothes from two days ago.

"Now, Peter Malvo. Thank *you* for joining us this morning."

"I didn't have much choice. Your dog there—" He points to Rob and leans forward in his chair. "Insisted I come speak with you."

"Alright, so tell me what I need to know about you and the Crimson Bears." Mr. Hudson leans back in his chair with his hands folded over his chest.

"Your suspicions were correct that I'm a new member of their crew. I'm actually the second-in-command's eldest son, but that's not why I'm here. Your dog told me someone is targeting your daughter, but it's not us." He stands and adjusts his jacket, but Mr. Hudson doesn't move.

I've had about enough of the *I'm better than you attitude* this kid is sporting. I step forward, fully intent on pushing him back into his seat, but Mr. Hudson raises his hand to stop me. Peter smirks at me. My anger simmers right below the surface.

"How can I know for sure? You've been seen purchasing roses recently, and you have a history of stalking." Mr. Hudson sounds bored of this conversation. If he wanted fireworks, he should have let me make the man sit. Then we could have seen who the dog in this room really is.

"Yes, we've made roses our new calling card, but not in this case." He holds up his hands in defense. "We've tried kidnapping your daughter in the past. It failed epically. As much as we would love to watch your empire crumble, we're not dumb enough to try to take your daughter a second time."

Mr. Hudson ponders this for a moment and then leans forward, setting a hand on his desk and nodding to Rob.

Rob walks to Peter and takes hold of him, and Peter sucks in a breath.

"Fine. I believe you, young man, but if it turns out that you *are* involved, you'll have a war on your hands. A war I promise you will lose. Rob, show him off the property."

"Yes, sir." Rob rolls his eyes and then pushes Peter out of the office.

The Crimson Bears theory is out, but I want to know what other secrets they're hiding since they managed to keep their second-in-command's child hidden. Once this issue with Rachel is resolved, my new personal mission will be to uncover every one of those secrets. I will not be blindsided again.

"Please tell me you found something in those files," Mr. Hudson grumbles into his hands before spinning in his chair to face me.

"I did, sir." I hand him the folder and he opens it. "Mark Kirkland. He is an associate of mine and Rachel's gym training partner."

"And why do you think this man is involved?" His voice is flat as he looks over the file.

I proceed to tell him the story. From the lie, the half-threat Mark made, to the plan of fake dating that became something more. I watch as he takes in every detail, and I hope this is enough to convince him to look deeper into Mark. I wasn't planning to walk him through the details, but I'm confident that Mark is involved. I can swallow my pride if it makes a difference in *her* safety. She is what matters above all else.

"I agree Mark could be the person behind this. Message Rob to bring him in."

"Yes, sir." I pull out my phone and start to leave his office.

"One more thing."

I pause, and anxiety coils in my chest. I turn to face him, and he stands from his desk and crosses the room until he's standing in front of me.

"You tried to do right by my daughter by agreeing to partake in her lie. Thank you for your loyalty." He holds out his hand, and a soft smile forms on his face.

"I only want the best for her." I take his hand. His grip is firm.

"Good. Now, matters of the heart are difficult. You're a good man, Daniel, and I'll let you date my daughter." He pauses, and when he speaks again, the tone he uses cannot be mistaken for anything but a threat. "But if you hurt her in any way, I'll skin you alive and make you beg for death."

"I understand, sir."

"Good. Now go check on my daughter and make sure Mark is here before end of day."

I nod and leave his office.

He's going to let us be together. That's a bigger relief than I was expecting. Mark will be dealt with and then my girl and I can go out on a date that's as real as the moon and the stars.

When I get to the cottage, it's as silent as when I left. She must still be sleeping. I walk to the room, eager to wake her and tell her the news. She'll be downright elated that we don't need to be concerned about her father anymore.

"Rachel, baby. It's time—"

I slide the door open, and the bed is empty.

I rush to the bathroom. Also empty.

At her nightstand, I hope to find a note since I never got a call or text. But there her phone sits, still on the charger.

CHAPTER 13

RACHEL

"OKAY, I'M HERE." I ENTER the guard booth at the front gate, still in my pajamas and wearing my slippers. One of my father's security members turns from the camera monitors with a white envelope in hand. He's young and new. I think his name is Patrick.

"Sorry for the inconvenience this morning, but with the potential threat, I figured it would be best to open this in here." He hands me the letter.

My name is written with harsh lines, like the person who wrote it was in a hurry.

"It's not a problem. I just appreciate that you didn't open my mail for inspection first." I offer him a reassuring smile, then rip the envelope open.

I pull out the note written on lined notebook paper

and a picture falls to the floor. My heart sinks and fear encompasses me at the sight of the image.

Mark is tied to a chair, with his wrists bound to its arms, and silver tape covers his mouth. My stomach rolls as I lift the photo to inspect it closer. Deep purple bruises wrap around his right eye and cover his left cheek. His bottom lip is split and his eyes . . . his eyes show defeat, like he has accepted his fate.

"Here, take this!" A new sense of urgency washes over me, and I slam the photo onto the monitor desk and scramble to open the note.

> *He wanted what is mine, but he will live. The man who shared your bed last night won't have the same mercy.*
>
> *Meet me in Falcon Park at 10 p.m. alone and I'll let them both live, but if I see members of your security or crew, I'll put a bullet in your friend's brain and then yours.*

My breath leaves my lungs like someone has punched me in the chest. I collapse to my knees, unable to stand under the weight of knowing that somehow I've caused harm to Mark, that Daniel is now in grave danger because of me.

"Shit. Rachel." The guard hits his knees in front of me and starts looking me over. "Just breathe." He takes the note and reads it.

My chest tightens, and my breathing quickens.

I can't breathe.

Mark is hurt. I'm not safe. Daniel's life is at stake. My body is shaking and my vision blurs.

Is this my fault?

Tears stream down my face. I don't understand how we got to this point, but I can't let people get hurt because of me. Daniel can't die for me.

The guard is moving, but I can't see. Oh god, I can't breathe. A vice is locking me down from the inside out.

Strong arms wrap around me, and my first instinct is to fight it. I push against the hold and bellow out a loud sob.

"Shhhh, baby girl, I've got you . . . shhh." Daniel's soothing voice surrounds me, and I turn into his chest as my tears flow.

I'm not sure how much time passes or when the world stops feeling like it's collapsing in on me. But eventually my mind quiets and my chest isn't so tight.

"Thank you." My voice is hoarse from crying, and my body is heavy with emotional exhaustion.

"No need for that. I'll always be here for you, in the good, the bad, and the scary." He rubs a comforting hand over my back. "Patrick, I'm going to take her back to the cottage. Please bring this new evidence back to Mr. Hudson, and I'll call him when she's settled."

"Yes, sir."

Daniel stands from the floor and cradles me to his

chest. He walks us from the booth, into my home, and lays me on the bed with a gentle touch. I floated the whole way. I didn't watch anything as we moved. The only thing anchoring me to the earth was Daniel.

That's why I know, beyond a shadow of a doubt, that I have to go to that park.

The room becomes a hollow void when Daniel leaves it.

I hear him on the phone with someone, but I can't bring myself to listen.

I won't let anyone die for me. Mark doesn't deserve what's happening to him, and Daniel . . . I will gladly meet whoever this is if it means he will be safe.

Daniel returns to the room and settles on the bed beside me, wrapping me in his warm and secure embrace. My heart cracks and silent tears fall. I want so desperately to have the fairy-tale ending, but the reality is that it will never happen. I'm resolved to my fate. I'm going to Falcon Park, and whatever happens, at least Daniel will be safe. It's not like we'll have a future together either way. At least with this, I can guarantee *he* will have a future.

"You know I won't let anything happen to you, right?" he whispers next to my ear, and I snuggle into him further.

"I know. You always take care of me." My voice cracks and his hold on me tightens.

"And I will until my dying breath."

I turn my body and throw my leg over him to get as close to him as possible. I kiss him, savoring his taste, his scent, the way his lips dance with mine. I let my soul cry out to his, pouring all the love and sorrow I have into him.

I run my hand over his waist, then up his arms, counting every scar and memorizing the curve of his shoulders and the way his skin feels against mine.

A knock on the front door sounds, and Daniel groans as he stands. "I'll be right back."

I nod and turn to my pillow, trying to stuff the sadness away. I seem to be doing a lot of that lately.

While he's gone, I reach for my phone and pull up Meg's text thread.

> Hey, I need a ride tonight.
> This stays between you and me.

> Where to, captain?
> I'm assuming security can't know?

> Falcon Park.
> I'll sneak out the side gate and meet
> you around the corner on Lane Rd.
> 9:30. No security.

> Not gonna lie, you're freaking me out a
> bit. Should I bring my revolver?

I forgot Meg owned a handgun. I have no actual plan here, but a gun might even the score a bit. Hope fills my chest. Maybe my fate isn't sealed just yet.

Yes.

CHAPTER 14

RACHEL

THE GENTLE NIGHT BREEZE IS bitter on my arms, causing goosebumps to prickle over my skin as I jog with light steps to the east gate of the property. I should have grabbed more than a black zip-up hoodie, but I needed to be able to move easily.

I have to move fast. Daniel will be back at the cottage in a few minutes, and he'll sound the alarm to all the guards. This is my only shot to keep him safe.

Once I round the large oak tree, the gate will only be a few feet away.

"Shit," I hiss when I notice the armed guard.

I press my back to the old oak, praying I haven't been spotted.

I pinch my eyes shut, trying to listen past the loud

pounding of my heart in my ears. No one approaches or yells and relief floods my system.

I need another way out, but the only other possibility will mean a long run through the woods in the pitch-black.

Daniel's safety is worth it. I can do this. I will not fail.

Renewed determination fills my system, and I watch the guard, waiting for my opportunity to run to the west side of the property.

Now!

I bolt, my head on a swivel watching for anyone who may spot me. On the other side of the property, I duck behind the large hydrangea bush, looking for the loose bars on the fence that Simon and I used when we snuck out as teenagers.

I start trying the bars, and the three loose ones give way. Guilt grips my chest as I hold the bars. I sent Daniel to the main house for ice cream, claiming I needed to eat my feelings this evening. I quickly changed and slipped out as soon as he left. I used his loving and caretaking heart to my advantage. Hopefully he understands that I'm doing this for him, and he can forgive me.

I wiggle my body through the opening I've created and then replace the bars. If someone happens upon the hole, they'd know it was me, and I need as much time as I can give myself before they realize I'm gone.

God, please let me come back.

I face the edge of the woods and then bolt into the thick, mangled mess of trees, staying hidden as I round the property line. The closer I get to Meg, the more my heart aches. I only left a note for Daniel.

I'm sorry, but this was the best way to ensure your safety. I'll be back soon, and if not, please find the love you deserve.

I didn't say what I should've. I didn't tell him that he holds my heart . . . that I love him. It would have made all of this so much harder to actually do. Not only am I running through the woods at night, but I'm running directly to an unknown villain who will determine my fate—and the fate of two good men.

Reaching the road's edge, I grip my side as my lungs burn. I make it a point to stay in shape, but running the back edge of the property has never been something I've trained for. Meg's little red beater is running with the lights off just on the side of the road a couple feet ahead.

I yank the passenger door open and plop down in the seat with a huff.

"You ready?" She raises her eyebrows at me. She's dressed almost identical to me in all black, but she won't be leaving this car.

"Yeah. Did you bring your revolver?"

"It's in the glove box, but can you tell me why

you need it?" She puts the car in gear and then white-knuckles the steering wheel.

"You remember when I was taken by the Bears?" Her eyes widen as she glances from the road to me and back. "Someone else is trying to get to me, and I'm meeting them tonight—alone—to put an end to this."

"LIKE HELL YOU ARE!" She slams on the brakes, tossing me into the dash.

"Jesus, Meg!"

"You are *not* meeting some freak alone. I'm not going to lose you again." She's frantic, and I know I would be, too, if I were in her shoes.

"Meg." I look at my hands. "You have to let me do this. He'll kill Daniel if I don't, and who's to say he'll stop there?" A stray tear rolls down my cheek and I bat it away. "I won't lose the ones I love. I have to end this tonight."

The car is silent as we both sit with the weight of this.

Slowly, Meg starts driving down the road again.

"I'll come with you." Her voice is firm. Despite the dark, I see her nod, like she's confirming it with herself.

"You can't. He left me a note saying to come alone or he'll kill me."

I look out the window as the weight of the ticking clock weighs on me. For every second that passes, I get closer to finding out who's behind this.

"Fine. But damn it, Rachel, you better come back

to me within fifteen minutes, or I'll come find you myself—damn the consequences."

Her love warms me. I can always count on her, no matter what.

The rest of the car ride is silent, and five minutes later, we pull into the long drive of Falcon Park. A lone streetlamp lights the parking lot, and near the top of one of the hills in the middle of the park is a hooded figure, silhouetted by two others. The moonlight shines off them and my stomach turns.

There they are. These are the people who want me.

CHAPTER 15

DANIEL

"OKAY, I'VE GOT COOKIES AND cream, but I also grabbed the salted caramel swirl," I shout as I enter the cottage while balancing both containers.

After receiving that note, Rachel was a mess, and when she gave me something I could actually do for her that wasn't just holding her and reassuring her it'd all work out, I basically ran out the door. Seeing her so broken tore my heart out, and I was helpless to help her. It's just stupid ice cream, but sugar can soothe a hurting heart.

Rob and the security team conference-called me about our plan for the note. Over my dead body was Rachel going to that park, but Rob and Patrick were going to go scope it out and see if they could figure out who was behind the threat. I'm sure they've left by now, and hopefully we'll have some answers soon.

Mark doesn't deserve the hand he's been dealt, and I will do whatever I can to help him, but not at the expense of Rachel. As far as threats to me, I'd like to see them try. This is not the first time my life has been threatened, and it might not be the last. I just need to keep my girl safe and I'll be fine.

"Baby girl, where you at?" I yell when I don't see her in the living room where I left her.

The house is eerily quiet. Again.

"Rachel!"

Anger swells in my chest, and deep inside, I know.

I know she went to that stupid park. She never brought it up. Never talked about it. That should have been the first warning, but I was too focused on her emotional state after her panic attack.

I check the house. Her room—empty. Bathroom—empty. Dining room—empty. And on the kitchen counter is a fucking note. *Damn it!*

What was the point of the last three years if she's just going to hand herself over and get herself killed?

I read the note and my chest aches, but I can't feel that right now. I latch on to my anger instead. First, I'm going to save her ass. Then, she will have hell to pay.

I grab my keys from the counter and leave the cottage, slamming the door behind me hard enough the windows rattle.

If something like this happens again in the future, I'll tie her ass to a damn chair. I should have known. He offered her something she would've never refused: her friend's safety and my life to be spared.

In my car, I check my 9mm pistol over, slam in the magazine, and lay it on the passenger seat. Then I grab my phone and send a text to Rob that Rachel is most likely at the park.

What the fuck is my girl thinking?! I let my walls down, I risked my whole career, I gave her my fucking heart, just for her to end up dead? I don't think so.

I slam the SUV into gear and floor the gas pedal, hitting the gate button so it's open before I even get there. Once through the gate, I ignore all traffic laws. She has at least fifteen minutes on me, and I need to be there now.

Pulling into the park's lot, I instantly identify Meg's car—it's the only one here, and only one person sits inside. I slam my brakes, stopping directly behind her little red car, and when I'm out of my SUV, I stalk to her driver's side window.

I smack my hand on the roof and Meg jumps a mile high. She rolls down her window, eyes wide and nervous, as I'm sure fire burns in mine.

"Where the hell is she?" I growl.

"I don't know." Her voice trembles. "She left ten minutes ago following three guys over that hill." She points, and I push off the car, marching in the direction she'd indicated.

"Daniel, wait!" she yells, climbing from the car and wrapping her arms around her abdomen protectively. "She has my revolver. A-and there was a gunshot."

I nod, taking off in a sprint to the top of the hill as my stomach rolls at the idea of what that could mean. Megan doesn't deserve a thank-you. In my book, she's an accomplice to Rachel putting her life on the line.

Bang! A gunshot rings out, and my stomach hits the ground.

I want to vomit. *Please don't be hurt, please God, let her be safe.*

At the top of the hill, panic grips my chest. Two bodies lay on the ground, unmoving, and two others are struggling at the edge of the tree line.

CHAPTER 16

RACHEL

ON THE HILL, I LOOK back at Meg's car and grip the revolver—tight. I can do this. I will be okay and so will the people I care about.

The three figures turn together and descend the other side of the hill, clearly not wanting to be in sight of the lot. *Smart. They don't want witnesses.*

They're waiting for me at the bottom now.

I look back toward Meg one more time, then look up at the sky. "Daniel, I love you." My chest aches as I mutter the confession, but these feelings will only make what comes next harder.

I lock away all emotion for possibly the final time, straighten my shoulders, look forward at the three figures, and walk.

They will not break me.

They will not end me.

I will end them.

One step. Two. Three.

I walk, never allowing my eyes to leave them. When I'm a few feet away, my body turns to ice as I recognize the three men before me.

"Patrick. Rob." I stare at my guards and then the bruised man in the middle—Mark. "What's going on?" Confusion laces my tone as I assess all three of them.

"Glad you could join us, Rachel." Mark crosses his arms over his chest with a wicked grin.

Something is very wrong here.

In an instant, I know. They are not my saviors. They are the masterminds. Why else would they have led me out here?

I take a step back. "But I don't understand." I shake my head, stepping back again and preparing to bolt. "The beating, the photo, it was all fake?"

This changes everything.

"Patick, deal with this," Rob says and nods toward me.

I turn on my heel and run. My heart is racing in my ears as the revelation courses through me like a bolt of lightning. Arms wrap around me.

"Let me go, you bastard!" I shriek and fight against his hold, but he struggles me to the ground.

I am not a victim. I came here with every intention of returning to the man I love.

With a tight grip on the gun, I pull it from my pocket, jam it into the side of his throat, and pull the trigger.

The shot rings out.

Patrick grunts and spits blood in my face.

My pulse pounds in my ears and my head spins. Adrenaline rushes through me, but I'm frozen as panic takes its hold.

"Fuck!" Mark yells, and I'm grabbed from behind, but I only stare at the dead man as I'm lifted from the ground.

I just shot someone.

Pain bites at my wrist as my gun is knocked from my hand, snapping me from my trance.

Without another moment's hesitation, I throw my head back and smash Mark's nose. It releases a sickening *crack*, and he bellows, but I'm still being dragged back toward the edge of the woods.

"Damn it, Mark! You're my friend! Let me go!"

"Coming from the bitch who humiliated me *and* just broke my nose," he growls.

Rob laughs as I thrash, trying to find leverage, but I'm failing miserably.

Rob comes into view as Mark drags me further, and he holds up his hand. Panic is replaced by rage. Cold. Cruel. Rage.

I stare at the man who has worked for my family for years. Our top guard. The one who has ensured my safety and has now chosen to betray us.

"Rachel, Rachel, Rachel." He shakes his head at me and puts his hands on his hips. "You're smarter than I thought you were. I didn't plan on you bringing a gun." He steps forward, and I feel my nostrils flare. "Too bad you wasted your shot on the lacky." He shrugs.

"What's your plan here, Rob?" I spit the words like acid, still trying to shake out of Mark's hold. We've been training partners for years; he knows my moves before I can even make them.

"Exactly what I told your father and Daniel: I plan to marry you, kill your father and brother, then seize control of the gang and assets. Then Mark here will get to keep you, since I'll have no further use for you." He pulls a gun from his pocket, and I plant my feet firmly. "Except it was never the Bears' plan. They were just an easy scapegoat." He rolls the gun around and points it at me.

I stare at the man I once knew as a close protector and steel my body not to give anything away. I now know he won't shoot me. He needs me. He just said as much.

Mark loosens his hold, and I shrug him off as I stare at the barrel.

"Now, you're going to do exactly as I tell you, or this bullet will go somewhere it probably shouldn't."

"What do you want me to do?"

"First, you're going to call Daniel and assure him you're okay. Then you're going to walk with me to the car on the other side of these oaks. Think you can handle that?" he mocks.

I nod and square my shoulders. I've yet to win, but like hell am I giving in without trying.

I whirl around and jab Mark straight in the throat. He gags and falls back. I tackle him to the ground, wrap my body around his, and pull him over the top of me to use him as shield. I snake my elbow over his throat and hold, tightening to close his airway. Pride fills me. Who knew outside the damn mat I'd kick his sorry ass?

"Put down the gun before I kill off your second-in-command here." I pull tighter to emphasize my demand as Mark gags again.

I came here to try to save him, because he was my friend, but *fuck*. He's part of the mastermind, and now, I don't hold any reservations about killing him myself. Hell hath no fury like a woman scorned.

"Here, I'll save you the trouble." Rob shrugs as the shot rings out and Mark's body jolts. Shock fills me as I stare, bug-eyed, as Mark gurgles on blood for a moment and then goes limp on top of me.

"WHAT THE FUCK?!"

In the moments that follow, all logic is simply gone. I manage to shove Mark's lifeless body off me, get to my feet, and charge straight at Rob.

CHAPTER 17

DANIEL

I'M RUNNING, BUT IT FEELS like a turtle could win this race. On the approach, I realize the first body is Patrick. *Shit.* Whoever this is got the drop on Rob and Patrick. I can't stop to check on him. I only assume that's Rob on the ground, too, and my girl is fighting for her life.

I push my body, willing it to move faster. Sweat prickles down my neck and my lungs burn. Her scream fills the air, and rage burns deep in my chest. She is mine, and nobody will hurt her and live to talk about it.

Finally, I'm close. It's Mark on the ground—dead. Rachel struggles but loses the upper hand as she's turned to face me with a gun pressed to her temple.

"Let her go." The words vibrate out of me in a deathly snarl.

I've felt anger so many times in my life, but this . . . this, as I stare into the sinister eyes of a once-trusted colleague, is a whole new level of pure, cold, calculating rage.

He's just as responsible for keeping Rachel safe as I am, but now he's chosen this, and he'll pay for his betrayal in blood.

"I can't do that, Daniel." Rob sneers and grips her tighter.

Rachel squeaks in pain, but I can't look at her. If I do, I'll lose the little thread of control I have, and she needs me to be at the top of my game now more than ever.

"If I let her go, then there's nothing stopping you from killing me."

I clench my fists, watching every slight move he makes, reading to see what his body will unintentionally reveal.

"Let her go, and I'll let you leave this park alive."

He cocks his head.

"It won't stop the manhunt coming for you, but it will at least give you a head start." I raise my hands, trying to seem nonthreatening.

He twists her to his side and takes a more aggressive stance in front of me.

"What kind of an offer is that!" he shouts as he steps forward with her. "With her as my hostage and eventually my wife, I'll be untouchable!" He lets out a deep and cocky chuckle. But that's his weakness. His confidence.

I step closer to him, only about a foot from arm's length of him. "If that's the plan, then what's stopping you from killing me and just moving on?" I challenge.

"Daniel, no!" Rachel cries out, and my chest aches.

"You're right. Nothing." He pulls the gun off Rachel and extends it in my direction just as I was hoping he would.

I smack the gun from his hand and charge at him. Rachel is tossed out of his grasp as I tackle him to the ground and land a blow straight to his cheekbone.

Rob growls and rolls us sideways, trying to land a punch of his own, but instead hits the ground.

He throws another, this time connecting with my jaw, and pain explodes through every nerve ending, but I swallow it.

I shove him off me, and when we're both on our feet, I rush him.

Taking his head in my hands, I drive my knee to his face. He stumbles backward.

"Fuck!" Blood pours from his nose.

"I'm just getting started, asshole."

I advance on him, swing low, and hit his ribs, and he curls in on himself, wincing.

"You stalked and mentally tormented her."

I jab his cheek, and he falls back to the ground.

"I watched you hurt her on this hill."

I climb over him and look down at his rung-out body. Then I grab his shirt and lift him off the ground.

"You held a gun to her head and threatened to kill her."

All I see is red as I land a blow to his jaw.

"Daniel!" Rachel shouts, and I look over at her distraught face. My anger starts to dissipate as I take her in. "Please. That's enough."

I let Rob fall back to the ground, but she's wrong. He hurt her. No amount of beating will be enough of a punishment for what he's done.

I retrieve his gun from where it lays in the grass and pick it up. When I return to him, I point it directly at his forehead.

"You know," I say as I hover above him, "for the betrayal, I'd love nothing more than to see how inventive Mr. Hudson would be in that basement of his. I'd even love to help him do it. But for the sake of my sweet and hope-filled girl, who I love, I'll give you the mercy of killing you in this park."

His face contorts into a jagged snarl as he spits at my feet. "Enjoy being a fucking dog the rest of your—"

Bang!

I don't linger at his dead body; justice has been served.

Instead, I rush over to Rachel and drop the gun to the ground.

I grasp her face in my hands as a sob racks through

her, and I pull her to my chest. With her safe in my arms, relief fills me. I hold her, savoring her warmth, stroking her back. I can't believe I almost lost this—almost lost her.

She is the sun in my dark life, and she has been for a long time, and if Rob had been successful . . .

My mind goes blank, the pain behind that thought too great. Failing her was never an option.

Pulling her back from my chest, I cup her cheek and swipe the lingering tears away. "Are you hurt?"

"Nothing but a few bruises." She sniffles and her eyes drop to the ground. "Daniel, I-I didn't . . . I needed to keep you safe," she sputters and looks up with love dancing in her tear-pricked eyes. "I couldn't lose you and I was so scared!"

"I know, baby girl. I felt the same way."

I pull her close to me again as Meg comes barreling down the hill toward us.

"Mr. Hudson called!" she yells frantically and out of breath. "I told him what was going on, and the rest of the team is on their way. Shit is that, Rob?" Her eyes go wide, and I can only hope that she has a strong stomach.

"Yeah. Let's get out of here. The team can deal with the bodies."

Meg nods nervously, and I take Rachel's hand, unable to feel secure in her safety if I cannot physically assure myself that she's there with me. We walk back up the hill, leaving Mark, Rob, and Patrick's bodies lying in the grass. It's a shitstorm to clean up but it's not mine. This woman right here, however, is mine.

"Now I'm only going to say this once, baby girl. If you ever do something like this again, I'll tie you to a chair every time I have to leave your side."

Meg looks over at me from my side and then jogs the rest of the way to her car, not wanting any part of my wrath.

"I did it for you," Rachel whispers.

"I know, but it's my job to keep you safe, not the other way around." I sigh as my chest aches with the reminder that I almost lost her. "I can't handle a world where you don't exist."

The image of that gun held to her head will fill my nightmares. She has gone from my client to the woman I secretly pined for to my entire world. I would burn everything to the ground if it meant she would be safe in my arms at the end of it.

"I can't either," she whispers and cuddles into me closer, and now I know I'm her world, too.

"I never did tell you, sweetheart. . . ."

She stops walking and I meet her eyes.

"Your dad gave his blessing for us to be together."

Her eyes search mine and slowly grow big and bright.

"When did that happen?" her voice starts to lift with shock.

"Right before you went to the booth for the note.

I didn't say anything because I wanted the time to be right—"

I'm cut off by Rachel crashing into me and slamming her lips to mine.

Time stops.

There is only this moment with her.

The cool breeze blowing around us, the sensual movement of our lips, the feel of her against me. This is worth every hardship to get here.

We break apart, catch our breath, and begin walking once more, taking our time.

One question gnaws at me.

"Would you still have come here tonight if I would have told you earlier?"

Maybe she wouldn't have risked so much if I had said all this sooner.

"Yes." She says without hesitation. But then she pauses and releases a heavy breath. "I came here tonight to save your life. That wouldn't have changed."

I crack my neck at her confession, but I withhold the frustration, because my chest swells knowing she loves me as I do her.

When we reach the SUV, we spot the rest of the security team's vehicles entering the lot. I usher Rachel into my passenger seat and shut her inside, blocking her from all the questioning that's about to unfold.

Mr. Hudson is the first to approach, with security and Night Stalker members close behind. I know I failed to keep her out of harm's way, but I kept her alive and that's what matters, so I square my shoulders and stand tall.

"Where is my daughter?"

"In the car and safe. Rob seemed to be the ringleader in this whole thing—"

"Is he secured? I plan to bleed that fucker for this." He snarls.

"No, sir, he's dead at the bottom of the hill along with Patrick and Mark, who were all members of this coup."

He snaps his fingers and nods in the direction of where the bodies lay, and five members take off, no doubt to dispose of the bodies before the police get involved. He sighs heavily, produces a cigar from his jacket pocket, lights it, and takes a long drag.

"You did good, Daniel. You kept my daughter alive and ended it all. I wish you would have left Rob for me, but that's not what's important here." He pauses to take another drag as I watch him closely. "Since there's now an opening, I'd like you to consider being my second."

"Sir—"

"Enough of that." He waves his hand at me. "You're dating my daughter, my little princess, call me John."

"Okay . . . John," I say it, testing the way the word feels in my mouth. "I'll consider your offer."

He nods, taking another drag and glancing at the

SUV behind me. "Bring my daughter to see me in the morning and I'll expect your answer then."

He claps my shoulder twice and then heads toward the hill.

Megan climbs out of her car after Mr. Hudson—John—clears the area and crosses her arms over her chest.

"What, Megan?" I'm sure I sound as frustrated as I feel. It'll take a while before I forgive her for her part in this.

"She's my best friend. If I didn't give her a ride, she would have come alone."

"I know, but you should have told me her plans."

She scoffs at me and then leans against her door.

"I couldn't betray her trust like that, and I know you're no idiot. You showed up just like I knew you would."

I scowl at her only because she's right.

"Fine, but if something like this ever happens again and I find out you helped her, there will be hell to pay, Megan."

She scoffs again and gets back in her car, leaving her door open to look back at me. "That's a price I'll gladly pay, Daniel." And she slams the door.

I roll my eyes and walk back to the driver's side of the SUV. Megan and Rachel would do anything for each other, and that's a quality I normally love. But tonight it proved it can also be a huge pain in the ass.

Once I'm in my own driver's seat, I look over at my dirty and tired girl. She smiles at me softly, and I lean over to kiss her gently.

"Thank you for the rescue." She says it softly.

"You're mine, baby girl. I'll always rescue you." She leans over and rests her head on my shoulder as our hands find each other and fingers intertwine. I throw the SUV into gear and drive us back to the cottage house. Her head never leaves my shoulder.

CHAPTER 18

RACHEL

THE MORNING SUN SHINES IN from my bedroom window, waking me to a dull ache in my head and stiff joints. Last night was real, I know it was, but somehow it still feels like some horrible dream.

I watched Mark die, I killed Patrick, I almost died. . . . I worry it will take a lifetime to feel like my hands are clean of the blood, but I'll have Daniel to help. I was successful. I saved him and, in return, he saved me.

I roll over to find Daniel sleeping peacefully. He was mad, but the main takeaway, for me, was how much he loves me. I brush my hand through his thick, brown hair and notice a couple grays starting to pop up. The sight of them makes me smile. My wolf is such a warrior, my warrior, and these are badges of honor for him.

He groans and stirs, then rolls, wrapping me in his strong and perfect arms. His eyes lazily open, and a loving smile instantly forms on his perfect lips.

"Good morning," I coo at him and run my hand through his hair once more.

"Good morning. You sleep okay?"

"Perfect with you next to me."

He moves as fast as lightning, pulling me under him as he towers over me. My core instantly goes molten. He leans in and kisses me hard, pressing his morning wood into me. I let out a needy moan, but he pushes himself off me.

"As much as I would love to enjoy you for breakfast, your dad would like to see us first thing." He gets out of bed, and I roll to enjoy his perfect body.

"He can wait. Come back to bed with me."

He slides his pants on and crawls back onto the bed, kissing me gently.

"No." He leaves the bed once more, and I sit up in annoyance. "Consider this your punishment for leaving last night."

I smack my hands on the bed. "Punishment! I did that for you. For us!"

He grabs his shirt from the floor and waves it at me as he leaves my bedroom. This is ridiculous. I jump from the bed in nothing but my panties and tank top and jog out to him in the kitchen.

"Daniel, you can't be serious right now."

He turns around and finishes sliding on his shirt, and his eyes rake over me hungrily. He wants me just as much as I want him, and if I'm not careful, this will turn into a battle of the wills, and I will definitely lose.

"Oh, I'm serious, sweetheart." He walks up to me and tips my chin so I'll meet this eyes. "Now go get dressed like you're told, and I might let you come later. . . . But if you want to argue, I can tease you all day and all night while you work on that paper for biology that you never finished—don't think I don't know about that. And then I'll leave you a horny mess tomorrow while you sit in your classes."

My jaw drops, and I cross my arms over my chest. "Oh, I feel like I will more than qualify for an extension on my homework since I was *held at gun point*, Daniel."

"Sweetheart, I'm sure that your professors would give you that, but *I* won't let you slack. You're lucky you didn't have classes the past two days—I would've still made you go."

I roll my eyes at how ridiculous he's being.

"Now be a good girl and go get dressed, or I will follow through on your consequences."

A threatening smile forms on his face, and I want to push every last one of his buttons.

I narrow my eyes at him. "You wouldn't dare, Wolf."

"Try me, baby girl." He pecks my nose with a kiss, but I turn on my heels to go get dressed. Deep inside,

I know he's a man who follows through on his threats and I don't want to test him.

Moments later, I'm standing before him in a flowing red miniskirt and a white tank top. He glares at me, and I only bat my eyelashes at him.

He won't touch me as "punishment," so it's only fair we both hurt, and Dad won't think anything of an outfit I've worn many times.

"Are we going?" I ask with a little attitude.

Daniel steps forward, close enough to the point we're almost touching. "I know what you're trying to do."

"I have no clue what you're talking about." I look up at him and give him a half smile.

"Mhmm." He rolls his eyes and walks to the door, opening it for me.

I head out, swinging my hips back and forth as the wind lifts the skirt's ruffles slightly. Daniel is next to me a moment later with a hand gently on my back.

"You're going to be the death of me," he whispers against my ear, and butterflies take flight inside. He may as well just say I love you. . . .

We approach the porch steps and Daniel opens the door for me.

"In here!" my dad shouts from the den off the entryway. He's in his favorite black leather armchair, sipping on a cup of coffee while looking out at the gardens. On mornings like this, he reminds me of the carefree father

I had as a child. He protected us from the ruthlessness of his work until we were much older. "Take a seat."

Daniel and I sit together on the gray sofa, and Daniel places a hand on my bare knee, not helping the hungry beast inside me.

"So, I'm assuming you have an answer for me?" Dad asks, and I turn to look at Daniel with furrowed brows and a cocked head.

"Yes, I'll accept, with the condition that I will remain Rachel's primary guard, and in the event that the demands of the role pull me away, I get final say on who will be guarding her in my absence." Daniel sits straight, and I'm beyond lost.

"What role?" I ask, looking between both of them.

"I asked Daniel to be my new second." He smiles at me and my jaw threatens to drop. That is a *huge* promotion and responsibility. "And I accept those terms. Now Rachel, I have some questions for you."

Oh, great here we go. One of my dad's lectures.

"Are you happy with Daniel?"

I pause, taken aback by his question, and I look to Daniel. "Yes, I'm happier than I thought possible."

"Okay, then, I won't pretend that I'm thrilled about my daughter dating a man fifteen years older than her, or that it all started from some game of charades, but love blooms in the most unique ways."

He stands in front of me and takes my hands. I stand to meet him, and he smiles at me the way he always does.

"As long as you're safe and happy, that is all that matters to me."

I wrap my arms around him, and he hugs me back.

"Thank you, Dad."

"Sure. Now one last thing."

I pull back and join hands with Daniel, who is now standing, too.

"If you ever run away to meet a person stalking and threatening you again, I'll find you first and lock you in the damn basement until the person is found. Understand me?"

Daniel starts laughing. "I already threatened to tie her to a chair."

"Good man." Dad chuckles.

I roll my eyes at both of them. "Okay, on that note, can I leave now?"

Dad kisses me on the cheek and nods at Daniel.

"Sure, enjoy your day, Princess."

I hug him again and then run out the door before I get called back.

Daniel is behind me in a second, and I giggle, dashing around a tree, turning it into a fun little cat-and-mouse game. I dodge him until finally I'm scooped up and thrown over his shoulder, and he smacks my ass hard.

"Hey!" I squeal while being carried to the cottage house.

"Hey, what? I caught you, didn't I? Now I'm claiming my prize."

"Oh, really?" I smile.

He hauls me into the house and tosses me onto my bed like a sack of grain. He stalks around the bed and heat floods me in anticipation.

He pulls his shirt off and stands at the foot of the bed, looking at me. Drinking me in as I do the same.

"Baby girl, I'm not going to fuck you."

My gut pangs in disappointment as soon as the words leave his mouth.

"I'm going to make love to you, because I do." He grabs my ankles and rips me toward him. He towers over me, mere inches from my face. "I love you with every fiber of me."

"I know, and I love you."

He kisses me deep and hard, pouring his love and passion into it, as I pour mine right back. He is my bodyguard, a sweet indulgence I should have never had, and now he is mine.

ABOUT THE AUTHOR

Nichole Steel is a spicy romance author who lives in West Michigan close to Grand Rapids. She loves to write morally gray men who are obsessed with their women, and all of her stories have some darker tendencies to them. Outside of her creative space, she enjoys connecting with people and the world around her.

Nichole's short story "Cupid's Crooked Arrow" appeared in *Craving You: A Spicy Valentine's Day Anthology*, in January 2025, and was released as a standalone ebook by Attic Ebooks shortly after. She is also the author of *Little Bird*, the first book of the Seattle Underground series, released in March 2025.

You can find Nichole on:
Instagram @nicholesteel.author

Learn more at:
bio.site/NicholeSteel

ACKNOWLEDGMENTS

I am so excited to have this novella out! This one was so much fun to write and I truly let my characters go a little wild. My publishing journey continues to be just that—a fun adventure with constant growth and learning.

First, I want to thank my amazing ARC readers from my first novel, *Little Bird*. Thank you for helping me title this novella! You will forever be a part of this story for me.

Also, I need to say thank you to my publisher, Nicole Frail. You continue to help me grow into a better author and thank you for believing in me enough to publish this! I was smacked by major life changes in the middle of the publishing process, so thank you even more so for your personal love, support, and patience with me in this, as well.

Next, I want to thank my mom. Thank you for being my biggest cheerleader in every step of my publishing career—from the long nights of edits to the crazy plot line talks—I love and appreciate you!

Lastly, thank you to my amazing readers! Without you, my dream would have never become a reality. I love and appreciate each one of you. I hope you had fun and enjoyed *Twisted Indulgence*.

ALSO AVAILABLE

CUPID'S CROOKED ARROW

Baker and booktrovert Zoey has every intention of being alone this Valentine's Day, but she finds herself standing uncomfortably in a nightclub instead. Soon, she catches the eye of the co-owners, Jagger and Nathan. With these powerful men at her side, Zoey's night has gone from reading a romance novel to being in one, filled with new experiences and hot endings . . . oh, and there's frosting.

Available as an e-book.
ISBN: 978-1-965852-26-2

CRAVING YOU

In this steamy Valentine's Day anthology, passion and longing are the driving forces behind every meal shared, every sweet treat baked, and every dinner course served. Whether you partake in the holiday or treat it as just another day, these twelve stories invite you to explore how food can bring people together and enrich sensual relationships on one of the most romantic days of the year.

Available in paperback & e-book.
Print ISBN: 978-1-965852-13-2
Ebook ISBN: 978-1-965852-10-1

LITTLE BIRD

Chelsey
Fairy tales don't exist in the mafia world. My father taught me that well. The only thing he loves about me is the price he gets selling me to the head of the Italian Mafia as a concubine. Desperate, I fled to Seattle for a chance at a new life. But the Romano brothers found me. Now to have the life I want, I will have to escape my captors—my strong, powerful, hot-as-hell captors.

Nico
We intend to keep her but that won't be easy. We've taken her to spite our biggest rival, but we didn't expect her to change everything. When danger strikes, we'll protect what's ours. No one takes what belongs to the Romanos.

Available in paperback & ebook.

Attic Books and Attic Ebooks
are imprints of Nicole Frail Books, LLC,
an independent ("indie") publishing
company located in Avoca, Pennsylvania.

Attic Ebooks is a digital-first imprint and is
open to submissions of various lengths,
including short stories and essays and
novellas. If the length and market allows,
longer works are considered for print with
Attic Books.

To learn more about submitting a query to
Attic Ebooks, visit www.attic-ebooks.com.

Readers!
Join the NFB Street Team for exclusive first
reads and swag from Attic & Attic Ebooks!
www.nicolefrailbooks.com/street